TAKEN IN FRONT OF HIM

TEN TIGHT LITTLE PRINCESSES STRETCHED BY THE BLACK BULL

AMBER GRAY   CHARLOTTE STORM

CONNIE CUCKQUEAN   ELIZA DEGAULLE

KIMMY WELSH   PHILLIPA SAINT

SAFFRON SANDS   STEPH BROTHERS

ZOE MORRISON

DISCLAIMER

All characters and events are entirely fictional and any resemblances to persons living or dead and circumstances are purely coincidental. All sex acts depicted occur between characters 18 years or older.

CONTENTS

About Shameless Book Deals   v

1. Blacked by the Landlord by Connie Cuckquean   1
2. Get Black by Steph Brothers   19
3. Cucked by the Black Boss by Eliza DeGaulle   39
4. Taming a Black Bull by Kimmy Welsh   64
5. All In by Phillipa Saint   82
6. Deep Dark Desire by Saffron Sands   104
7. The Proposal by Amber Gray   121
8. On the Prowl Again by Zoe Morrison   140
9. A Neighbor in Need by Sharra Somers   169
10. Daring the Professor by Charlotte Storm   184
    Shameless Book Deals   206
    More from Shameless Book Press   207

Get Free Erotica Downloads at Shameless Book Deals

Shameless Book Deals is a website that shamelessly brings you the very best erotica at the best prices from the best authors. Sign up to our newsletter to receive the following benefits from an erotica recommendation service with a difference:

Highly Specific Recommendations: Our system has been put together from the ground up so as to not lump all erotica under a single umbrella. While the service is gathering speed, a combined recommendation service is necessary, but as time goes on, our recommendations will get more specific based on erotica sub-genres, or kinks if you prefer. You choose the erotica sub-genres you want. We are the first to do this on such a scale.

Discreet: Although we are shameless we are also discreet. Our emails go straight to your inbox and our email subject lines will not be overly crass or vulgar. Graphics in our emails will be almost entirely book covers, more closely vetted than the eBook retailers are able to achieve. That said, the emails will be filled with erotica recommendations, so don't gather your friends and family around the computer when you read them if you don't want everybody to know what blows your hair back.

Professional: Shameless Book Deals is run by Scarlett Skyes, a #1 erotica author with an eye for quality erotica.

Quality: All authors/publishers are expected to hold to a high standard for their work and the deals they are offering to our subscribers. Check the Newsletter Submission Guidelines and report any authors that you believe have breached these guidelines. We recognize that not all complaints will be valid, but authors/publishers who are repeat offenders will be blacklisted to maintain the quality of our service.

Free Stories: Every subscriber gets access to a selection of FREE, and in some cases exclusive, erotica. Downloadable directly from our website.

BLACKED BY THE LANDLORD BY CONNIE CUCKQUEAN

When the rent is due Kelly's husband Blake—who fancies himself a businessman—tries to negotiate the payment in a different form altogether. Black landlord Trevor isn't the kind of guy to be messing with. When Blake's plan is discovered Kelly's determined to make him regret it. Read how black bull Trevor takes his prize while Blake watches on, utterly cucked.

~

*M*aking rent had always been a challenge for Blake and his wife Kelly. She worked in the laundromat across the street whenever they had shifts for her, and it was there that she'd sometimes see Trevor, her landlord.

"Morning," he said one day, looking somewhat suspicious to Kelly as he came into the shop without a laundry-load.

"If it isn't my favorite landlord," she said, smiling broadly. Kelly knew enough to know that you needed to stay on the good side of someone like Trevor.

He walked up close to her, his tall, strong frame shadowing her from the outside light. Kelly felt her heart quicken. She could smell the woody scent of his aftershave. His muscle t-shirt was pulled tight across his chest and his dark, caramel face seemed serious.

"What's up?" Kelly asked, suddenly wishing she wasn't alone.

"There's something I gotta tell you," he said, rubbing at the short stubble of his face.

"What is it?"

Trevor looked suddenly vulnerable and Kelly's fright turned instead to compassion.

"Oh, God, what is it?"

She rushed to the door and turned the 'Open' sign over, bolting the lock.

"It's your husband," Trevor began.

"Jesus, what's he done now?"

"Well, your rent this month is late and…"

"That asshole!" Kelly blurted. "You know he's been *investing* most of it? He wastes it on these stupid online projects and—"

"It's not that," Trevor interrupted, and again he looked pained to continue. "He offered me something. Something instead of money."

She breathed heavily, her big tits pushing against her tight, checkered button-up. She brushed her blonde hair behind her shoulders and tried to calm herself.

"What?" Kelly asked, confused now.

Trevor reached into his pant pocket and pulled out his phone, brushing his thumb over the screen. Silently he turned it towards Kelly and held it in place.

Her blue eyes scanned the screen and as she did Trevor watched them narrow and her brow furrow in anger.

"That fucking *asshole*!"

"I thought you should know."

"Has he sent you any videos yet?" Kelly asked, eyes wide in panicked curiosity.

"No," Trevor said, and he brushed his chin again and looked up and down her petite frame.

"Thanks for letting me know," Kelly said.

"No problem. I hope you work things out."

Trevor turned the sign back over and unbolted the door.

"Trevor," Kelly said suddenly.

He spun around to look at her. Kelly was now leaned back against the table with an extra button undone on her plaid shirt. He froze, but his gaze didn't falter.

"Would his plan work?"

A twinkle sparkled in Trevor's chocolate-brown eyes. "I'd need a little more than just naughty videos of you."

He pulled open the door and walked back across the street, entering the four-story apartment building that he owned.

Kelly mused. The anger she felt towards Blake was unrivaled. She wanted to get him back and hit him where it really hurt. A sinful idea started to blossom.

BLAKE TWISTED the key in the lock and pushed through the door into his apartment. He closed it behind him and turned, noticing his wife but not yet noticing the scowl scrawled across her face.

"Evening, honey," he said, putting down his briefcase that contained today's newspaper and not much else.

"Don't you fucking '*honey*' me."

He set his briefcase down beside his gray pant-suited legs and prepared for a fight. They were commonplace by now.

"Offering to send dirty videos of me to our fucking landlord!" she screamed, launching herself towards him and slapping his chest.

Blake held his hands up, peering through them and trying to block the next lunge.

"I'm enterprising!" he cried. "I thought I could strike a deal."

"*Enterprising?*" she yelled, and she took another swing for him. "Is that why you've been begging to record me every time we fuck?"

"Honey," he said again, biting his lip quickly after and anticipating a reaction.

Kelly's shoulders rose and dropped powerfully with each breath. Her jaw was tight and clenched and her otherwise cutesy tank-top looked suddenly like a fighting vest.

"That's how you pay the fucking rent?!" she swung again and hit his stomach.

Blake stepped out from the wall and spun away to the middle of the room with a hand on his white shirt where Kelly had clocked him and another one outstretched to fend her off.

"Come on," he said. "We can talk about this."

"Look where your talking gets you," Kelly cried, defiant. "You couldn't talk your way out of a paper-bag."

"I work hard for us," he said.

Kelly often wondered why she'd stuck with him. Blake was the first guy who'd shown a genuine interest, but now his potbelly and receding hairline weren't doing much to keep her around. His promise of change and the strange allure that he still held were the only things keeping her there now. She was gambling on Blake and Blake was gambling on their relationship.

"You work hard for yourself," she spat.

"We can't keep missing the rent. We'll be out on the street. Do you want that?"

There was a brief moment of calm as the eye-of-the-storm hovered above. Blake used it to bridge the divide between them, turning his voice soft. Kelly stared down at the floor.

"I don't want that for us, honey," he said, lifting her chin.

Kelly looked beyond him.

"I don't want us to lose this place," he said, stroking a thumb at her soft skin.

"We won't," Kelly said with absolute certainty.

"That's the spirit," Blake said, and he brought her in for a hug.

She pushed back and raised her voice. "We won't because I've done my own negotiating instead."

Blake stood there, his hands at his side, confused. "Huh?"

Just then there came a knock at the door.

"And here it is now," Kelly said.

She walked towards the door and opened it wide, standing behind it and presenting the visitor to Blake who stood across from the threshold.

"Trevor?" Blake said.

Trevor's big desert-boots thudded on the hardwood floor as he entered the room. The mood of the place changed instantly.

"Have you spoken to your wife?" he asked, his voice deep and commanding.

"I—I—about what?"

Trevor looked to Kelly and tilted his head, nodding to Blake. "Tell him."

"I've been *enterprising*," Kelly said.

Blake looked between the pair of them.

"You've got something Trevor wants," Kelly said. "And I've negotiated a deal for it."

"What's that?" Blake said. The shoe was firmly suspended above him, reluctant to drop.

Trevor walked into the room and closed the door behind him.

"Me," Kelly said, and she walked a couple of paces and draped herself on Trevor's thick frame.

Blake's face twisted in confusion. "You? Him?"

"Free rent for the rest of the year," Trevor said.

"That's great!" Blake gushed, not yet realizing the consequences.

"Free rent," Kelly repeated. "And all I have to do is get fucked by this handsome stud." She rubbed her hand over the white t-shirt that bound Trevor's caramel flesh. "Good deal, huh?"

"What the fuck?"

"Sounds like a good deal to me," Kelly said.

"Me too," Trevor agreed, looking down at her. Kelly reached her lips up to him and kissed him.

"Kelly!" Blake cried.

"What?" she shrugged. "You were auctioning off my body anyway. I just thought I'd get the most for my pussy that I could."

She reveled in the torment that riddled Blake now. Too proud to admit he'd been stupid—too weak to do anything about it.

"This is a fucking joke," Blake said, and he moved to leave.

Trevor put his hands against the door as Blake pulled it.

"There was one other condition," Kelly said.

Blake took his hand away and looked sheepishly at Trevor.

Kelly dropped the cherry on the cake. "You have to watch."

It was something that would have broken most couples, but then it seemed Blake and Kelly weren't like most. Trevor spotted it in Blake's eyes before Blake even knew he was going to agree to it. He was a businessman—self-styled—but the deal sounded good to him.

"Alright," Blake said. Kelly was taken aback by his acceptance.

"You're gonna watch?" she asked.

"Might as well," Blake shrugged.

Trevor pulled Kelly's arm and tugged her towards the couch. She locked her eyes on Blake as the big bull pulled her away from him. He looked downbeat and humiliated.

"I wanna fuck you on here," Trevor said, and he tossed her to the couch like a piece of meat.

Kelly shrieked with frightened glee. Trevor seemed a totally different guy to the caring protector she'd spoken to in the launderette.

He rubbed at the crotch of his jeans and Kelly watched in awe as something huge awakened beneath.

"Sit here, businessman," Trevor said, looking back to Blake who looked to have shrunken in size.

He walked timidly towards the chair and Trevor waited patiently, his t-shirt pulling tight over his barrel chest every time he inhaled.

Kelly sat on the couch in a pair of tight, black yoga-pants and a white tank-top, waiting as Blake shuffled to his seat.

He sat down carefully, taking a deep breath as he realized that this might be a defining moment in his pathetic existence thus far.

"Good," Trevor said. With Blake in place Trevor lifted his t-shirt. Kelly's eyes were immediately drawn to the rippled abs that came out from underneath.

He pulled his t-shirt down his arm and his black marble pecs flexed. Trevor dropped onto the couch, putting a knee on the cushion beside Kelly and leaning over.

Kelly looked for cues as he approached. His hand rested

on her midriff and his lips came to hers. They kissed passionately and Blake watched on from his perch, helpless.

The only noise to be heard in that moment was the smacking of Trevor's lips as he tasted Blake's wife for the first time.

Blake watched awestruck. He was catatonic, enraptured on the chair. He hadn't expected to enjoy the sight so much, but something about a burly, muscled, black guy with his hands all over his wife was doing something for him.

He watched close as Trevor's shovel-like hand came up and squeezed his wife's big tits. She moaned in response and Blake felt a twitch in his pants as something awakened inside him.

Trevor pulled his mouth off Kelly's and the two stared into each other's eyes. The allure between the pair of them was undeniable.

She took a quick glance to Blake and then looked back to Trevor.

"Come get what you want," she said, and she reached out a hand to outline the huge packet that hung in Trevor's baggy pants.

The waist of his jeans hung below the waist of his tight boxer-shorts. The strap held tight to his skin, hugging the muscles and the Atlas cut of his body that seemed to point downwards into his pants.

Kelly's long-nailed finger teased at the flap of belt that encircled his waist. She pulled it out through the clasp and Trevor helped to open it up.

"That's what I want," she purred, and she leaned forward and popped open the button of his pants.

Blake's pupils fattened and his heartrate soared as he watched on. His hands gripped at the chair and his back was straight. It was difficult for him to admit to himself how much the sight delighted and humiliated him all at once.

Trevor barely looked at him. Instead his focus was on the beauty beneath him who was now frantically opening his pants as her desperation for his thick length intensified.

Blake's dick wasn't exactly small, unless you were comparing it to Trevor's. By contrast he was the rolling-pin to Blake's cigar-tube. Suddenly the thought of being satisfied by what Trevor had to offer was exciting Kelly.

She flashed down his zipper and pulled at his pants in desperation, leaning her head closer towards Trevor as though she demanded a front-row seat to the big reveal.

Trevor knew better than anyone what he was in possession of. He smirked downwards at the sight of yet another white woman, ravenous and desperate for the real deal.

He eased down his pants and took his boxer-shorts with them. They slid over his skin and suddenly Kelly spotted the coarse, kempt, black hair that thickened around the hilt of his shaft.

He was angled downwards for the moment, but Kelly could see the powerful sinews at the base of his cock that strained in their fight to defy gravity.

"My God," she swooned, breathless as inch-after-inch of thick, black chocolate was revealed to her.

Blake felt another pang of humiliation strike in his stomach. He felt queasy and yet, despite it all, his cock started to stiffen too.

Finally the tip of Trevor's cock was unshackled and it sprang upwards, striking Kelly's face as it did so.

She recoiled in shock and then started to giggle, marveling at the sight before her.

"It's so fucking big," she gushed, looking back to her husband. "Are you seeing this?"

Blake was quiet, watching carefully. He was seeing it all.

Kelly's delicate hand made a fist around the thick barrel

in front of her and Trevor exhaled, moving her hair aside and giving himself the best view possible.

"Swallow it," he said.

Kelly laughed. "I'll try."

Blake's mouth opened along with Kelly's as though he was eating too. She fought her lips over the bulbous crown and dropped a couple of inches of Trevor into her mouth.

He groaned appreciatively, sucking a breath through his teeth and smoothing his big hand over the blonde hair of his trophy.

Blake bit the inside of his mouth as he watched Kelly wind her lips over Trevor's prowess, struggling to fit more than about a third of him inside her.

"Good girl," Trevor said, and his hips started to pump slowly into her.

Kelly stayed put on the couch, leaning back into the cushion as Trevor moved forwards. With nowhere left to retreat she stayed in place. Trevor eased those few inches in and out of her slowly, building his breaths as he did so.

"Good girl," Blake whispered, leaning in to watch closer.

Kelly spotted her husband's sudden interest and she started to work harder, teasing more of Trevor inside her until her throat bulged with him and her eyes watered.

Her hands squeezed at his big, smooth balls, rolling them in her palm like a stress reliever and turning his black cock slick and glistening with her spit.

She gasped off him and a string of saliva webbed across her open mouth. She stared up at Trevor and his hands gripped her tank-top. He pulled it up over her head and Kelly's big tits fell out. Before now, Blake had been the only guy allowed near them.

"That's what I want," Trevor said.

Trevor fell against the couch and kissed Kelly again, moving down off her face and wrapping his thick lips over her pink nipples. His tongue circled her in the embrace and she quivered excitedly, feeling her sexuality awaken.

When his lips came away her nipples sat stiff and bullet-like, punching out from each breast and demanding the attention that her husband seldom gave her.

Blake watched on, his face a strange mix of curiosity, guilt, pain and excitement. At times he'd exhale loudly, as though it was all too much for him, but then he'd lean forward for a closer look, punishing himself for his stupidity.

Kelly looked down her naked chest at Trevor as he mouthed over her tits. His big, pink tongue slathered her chest and she felt the tremble of arousal in her pussy as the juices came to the fore. If she was to have any hope of hosting Trevor, she needed to be wetter than ever. Thankfully, Trevor was well versed in getting a woman worked up.

He kissed down off her chest and Kelly marveled as he continued lower. Blake was a stranger to cunnilingus, but here was his rival: willing to treat his beauty to untold pleasures.

His mouth kissed at her crotch and he bit at the stretched fabric, pulling it away from her pussy as Kelly looked down. Her pupils were fat with excitement. She didn't want to miss a thing.

Trevor gripped at either side of her crotch and flexed. His muscles bulged in his arm briefly as the sound of tearing fabric penetrated the silence.

Kelly gasped, realizing in an instant that he'd just split open the front of her garment. Blake moved forward to the edge of his chair and Trevor remained unfazed, kissing now at the thin strap of panties that covered her modesty.

"Yes, Trevor," she cried, closing her eyes and leaning back into the sofa-cushion.

Hearing his wife say another man's name made Blake's

stomach twist in a knot. His hard cock sat in his pants, embarrassing him further.

By now Trevor had turned the crotch of her panties wet. The red fabric darkened around her mound and Trevor started to bite at it and pull it back with his teeth.

Kelly took a look to Blake. She reminded herself of his initial plan, banishing any guilt she might have felt. In an act of defiance she slid a finger beneath the crotch of her panties and pulled it aside, baring her wet flesh to Trevor.

"That's my pussy," he said then he tongued along the groove and enclosed it between his lips.

Kelly's eyes shut tight and she yelped with glee to the ceiling. Her bull's tongue slithered between her lips, parting the petals of her flesh like a biblical hero splitting the Red Sea.

Trevor ate ravenously, pushing his tongue into her honey-pot and making no bones about having Blake see everything. He even moved her hips to angle her pussy right towards her husband, then he came in from the side so that Blake could see the tormenting point of contact between Trevor's pink, pointed tongue and his wife's pink flesh.

"Take my jeans off," Trevor said suddenly, glancing only briefly at Blake before resuming his meal between Kelly's legs.

Kelly looked to him, wondering if he'd do it.

Blake cleared his throat as if he was about to speak.

"Take my jeans off, cuck" Trevor repeated, sterner.

Blake rose to his feet, defeated. He walked to the back of Trevor and deflated as he looked over Trevor's shoulder and into the pleasured face of his wife.

Kelly groaned, her big tits bunched together on her chest. Trevor's broad back led down to his athletic, toned ass.

Blake took grip of Trevor's jeans and pulled them down his thighs. Trevor cocked a knee off the floor and Blake helped his pants over them, then did the same to the other leg.

He took Trevor's boots off, straining to pull them off the heel. Trevor kept himself busy, smacking his lips over the wet flesh of Kelly's pussy as it drooled out her cum, ready for the final, humiliating act.

"Go sit back down," Trevor said to Blake, nodding to the chair.

Blake threw Trevor's jeans aside and walked away, having released his rival completely. Beneath his ebony body Blake could see that huge monolith, still stiff and pointing right to its prize. Kelly would feel it soon.

As Blake returned to his seat Trevor stood up. Kelly shuffled on the chair, wondering what she was supposed to do.

"Ready?" Trevor asked, holding his cock and jerking it slowly.

Kelly eyed it one last time and then looked up at Trevor's face. "Fill me with it," she dared.

Blake's head was in his hands as Trevor reached beneath Kelly's back and moved her effortlessly into position. Her legs fell open and the soaked mound of her flesh awaited Trevor's thickness.

He took his cock in his fist and pointed it towards its target. Blake peered through his fingers and watched his wife's face explode in pained ecstasy as the bulbous crown of Trevor's fat cock pierced her tight pussy.

"Yes!" she wailed, and the walls of the apartment shook with her cries.

Blake fell back in the chair, utterly defeated. All he could do now was watch.

"Take note, white-boy," Trevor said, looking back to Blake. "This is how you fuck your wife."

Blake said nothing.

Kelly breathed long and deep. The size of Trevor inside

her was like reverse childbirth. She did everything she could to try to relax around his size, but each time it pushed deep she was reminded of how inadequate her husband was.

"Every inch!" Kelly cried, keen not to waste her moment.

"That's it," Trevor said, seeming proud. "Take this big, black dick."

Trevor slammed against her, deep enough so that the flesh of his hips struck the white ass of Kelly, ringing out in an applause that Blake didn't share.

He looked on, unable to take his eyes off the scene. He had hoped to placate Trevor with photographs or perhaps a video, and yet here Trevor was, having the whole cake for himself with no intention of sharing. Kelly would be forever his after today.

Trevor pounded her over and over and Kelly wailed like a stuck pig. Each raucous cry was like a dagger to Blake's heart, yet still his cock remained hard. Against all odds the arousal just did not go away. There was something buried deep inside him that seemed to suggest that this wasn't humiliation at all—it was recompense.

Trevor's vice-like grip cradled Kelly again and this time he lifted her from the couch completely, putting to use each one of his finely sculpted muscles.

He took a half-turn with Kelly in his arms and her legs wrapped around his torso. She started to kiss him and Trevor faced her ass to Blake so he could see it all.

Kelly started to squeeze up Trevor's body, lifting her pussy off his cock just enough for Blake to be able to see underneath and through the tear in the fabric of her yoga pants.

He watched Trevor's shaft emerge, creamed up in a white film of his wife's love. He'd never managed to make her do that to his own cock.

Trevor tormented him for a few minutes longer, standing

proud and letting Kelly bounce against him. Eventually he turned again and sat himself down on the sofa, giving Kelly her position on top.

Her yoga pants stretched down her legs as she squatted over Trevor's cock. He reached his hands behind to her ass and fed his fingers into the rip, pulling again and stretching it open wider.

The fabric tore open and Kelly's big ass bounced free. The whole thing wobbled hypnotically as she began her canter, trotting up and down on Trevor's cock like he was a champion racehorse and she was the jockey.

This time Blake didn't need any instruction. As though he was fully aware of the punishment that he required, he moved his chair so that he could see the view right between their legs.

"Take it," Trevor snarled, looking up to his mistress. "Take my fucking cum in your pussy."

Those words were a death knell. Blake's soul damn-near left his body as they struck his ears. By contrast, Kelly was perkier than ever.

"I want it," she cried, bouncing up and down on his big cock like she was racing a pogo-stick.

Her tits swayed on her chest and Trevor looked up at the view, thanking his lucky stars that pathetic white guys like Blake existed.

"Tell me what you want," Trevor insisted, keen for Blake to hear her wish.

"I want your fucking cum," she said.

"Beg me for it," Trevor snarled, slapping her ass.

She wailed as he struck her, crying out the words with more venom. "Give me your fucking cum!"

Blake exhaled, rubbing at his crotch finally and giving way to the arousal that had tormented him so far.

His wife bounced, squeezing tight around Trevor's cock

that was coated in a glaze of pearly white. Each time she rose up her ass clapped around him, massaging the hilt before bathing him in the warmth of her soaking wet pussy.

Trevor squeezed her hips and Blake watched as the red outline of Trevor's slap drew itself on his wife's ass. To Blake it was like she'd been branded: proof positive that Kelly belonged to Trevor in that moment, and no-one else.

Blake rubbed his hand along his cock and lamented the choices that had brought him here. His wife found another gear and bounced faster, letting out her rallying cry.

"Come for me," she urged. "Come in my pussy. I want it! I want it! I want it!"

Trevor's legs straightened out and Blake's eyes grew wide as he watched. He could barely bring himself to blink. He knew that he deserved to witness this moment. He deserved to have front-row seats to the erupting, black length of the man inside his wife.

"Oh, fuck, baby," Trevor said, and a slither of his mystique was lost to his suddenly urgent words.

"Give it to me!" Kelly demanded, pinning Trevor down by his flat, hard stomach and bouncing her big ass on his pole.

Blake watched those black balls pull to the base of Trevor's cock and then a deep, booming groan escaped his lungs. It filled the room like an animal's roar.

"Fuuuuck!" he cried.

Kelly didn't stop. As Trevor's big cock twitched and let off its first bountiful rope of cum, she continued to ride him. Her ass slapped down on his thighs and gradually the white cum that dribbled over Trevor's cock belonged to him now and not her.

Blake marveled as Trevor's seed ran down his length like stripes on a zebra. He watched his wife's pussy sink down over it and reclaim his escaping seed, spreading it back up along that chocolate length that suddenly looked more appealing to Blake than ever.

Kelly was in no mood to stop. The broken groans that escaped Trevor told Blake that he still had plenty to give. Of course he did. It was only right that the guy was not only bigger, stronger and more well-endowed than Blake, but he also had a volume of cum that Blake couldn't even begin to compete against.

Finally Kelly could hold no more. It started to run freely out of her and drip onto their couch. Blake watched it fall, knowing that that particular piece of furniture would be tainted forever.

She slowed her bucks and hung her tits in Trevor's face as she hugged him close, grateful of his gift to her.

"That—was fucking—incredible," she breathed, giggling deliriously afterwards.

Blake's hand was still on his crotch now as he stared through the pair of them, looking into the middle-distance.

Kelly rose up with one last groan, releasing the cum-soaked cock of Trevor that slapped back heavily against his caramel stomach.

"Mmm," she groaned, and without prompting she sank her mouth to him and sucked the tip of his cock one last time.

Trevor stroked her hair and groaned, watching close as she cleansed all she could from him.

Blake, in contrast, sat silent, staring now into the smashed pussy of his wife. It was dappled with white cream that ran sticky from the gasping O of her sex.

Trevor's attention shifted to Blake fully for the first time as he watched him slide forward from his chair. Blake fell to his knees and crawled across the carpet, targeting his wife's exposed pussy.

"Shit," Trevor laughed, and he watched Blake dock onto the back of Kelly and begin to feed.

Kelly's eyes bulged and she closed them to groan. "Get his cum, baby," she said.

Trevor couldn't believe it. Kelly seemed to take it in her stride. She moved her hand and gripped the back of her husband's head, smothering it against the seed of his rival and refusing to let him up for air.

She turned to Trevor and smirked. "That ought to keep him busy."

With that she opened her mouth over Trevor's cock again and he groaned in disbelief. The stiffness of his dick waned, but it looked no less impressive.

Blake smothered his wife's flesh and tasted the bitterness of defeat in her pussy. He lapped hungrily, feeling that deep sense of guilty pleasure and letting the waves of humiliation wash over him, as though it was cleansing him of his wrong-doing. A baptism of cum.

"Good boy," Kelly said. "Good boy."

THE END

Get Access to over 20 more FREE Erotica Downloads at Shameless Book Deals

Shameless Book Deals is a website that shamelessly brings you the very best erotica at the best prices from the best authors to your inbox every day. Sign up to our news-letter to get access to the daily deals and the Shameless Free Story Archive!

GET BLACK BY STEPH BROTHERS

Douglas has been cheating on his wife, Eleanor, for about a year. Nothing serious—in his mind, at least—just one-nighters with anonymous women.

But one night, his gorgeous young wife turns up at his favorite pickup joint, dressed to kill, and changes everything. Because she's not there to catch Douglas...she's there to get back at him. She's meeting the towering, dark-skinned Ambrose—knowing full well her husband will be watching on.

With the tables turned, Douglas struggles to suppress his anger. But the longer he watches them, and the more intimate they get, the more his anger changes...to arousal.

～

I paused outside the door to O'Flaherty's and took a long breath, holding it in for a few seconds. As I let the air out, I slipped my wedding band into my pocket, and stepped through into the warm lighting and pleasant noise of people drinking and flirting.

The breath thing was a little ritual I'd developed, ever since I'd started cheating on Eleanor. It was like a cleansing process. The emptying of my lungs took the old Douglas with it. And the next breath in was filled with the atmosphere of my favorite Irish bar.

I was a whole new man; no wife, no backstory, no ties. Just a player named Armand, with an unquenchable need for new pussy.

Of course, I knew what an asshole I was being. Eleanor had always been good to me. A wonderful girlfriend who, two years ago, became a steady and loving wife. Hot as hell when we first started going out. Still cute as a button.

But she'd grown more and more distant, both emotionally and physically, for the past year or so. About as long as I'd been ritually cheating on her.

She'd suggested couples therapy a few times, but I was pretty happy with how things were. Therapy would get in the way of these fun nights of meaningless sex. I'd be trapped in a room with a stranger, and the woman who didn't want to fuck me anymore.

Did she grow cold because my cheating changed me? Or did I start cheating because she grew cold? I wanted to believe it was the latter, but it was more likely the former.

Anyway, it was one of those old chicken-and-egg things. And far too hard to think about when my cock was roaring at me to go land some tight, young pussy.

As I scanned the bar, my belly tightened. I had a lot of competition tonight. Men of all shapes, sizes and colors were scattered about the place. I was worried it was going to be a total wiener-fest.

A place opened up at the end of the bar, and I scooted over to order a whiskey. Turning my back to the barman, I scanned the place from my new angle, pleased to see at least a dozen hot prospects for me to target.

The sound of my glass being placed on the bar caught my attention and I swiveled to pick it up. As I turned back and took a slug, a change filtered through the place.

A quick glance at the entrance told me why. The most gorgeous young brunette had come in, wearing a ridiculously tight and short black dress, with thigh-high stockings and three-inch stilettos. Every man stopped what he was doing and stared at her, jaws heading south and cocks heading north.

I scanned her from those sexy shoes upward, taking in the athletic curves of her long legs, hovering at the delicious swell of her rounded hips. Up past those mouth-watering breasts, barely covered by the low-cut front of her dress. Past the sinful black choker that made me harder than theoretical physics, and up to her face. Her gorgeous full-lipped, wide-eyed face.

The face of my wife.

I spat out the mouthful of whisky I'd forgotten was in there. Thankfully, there was enough noise to cover me, and I slunk away from the bar and into the shadows. The last thing I wanted was for her to find me here.

Except...why the hell was Eleanor even in the place? Dressed up in clothes so fucking fine and sexy I hadn't recognized her at first. If she even thought about cheating on me, I'd...

Well, fuck. I had no moral high ground here, of course. But we all know it's different for men, right? We're constantly walking around, just a hair-trigger away from a hard-on.

So, we sometimes stick it where it shouldn't be stuck. That's just par for the course, right? It didn't mean anything, right?

Right?

From my hiding place in the shadows, I watched Eleanor

approach the bar. The sea of men parted before her as she sauntered over and ordered a drink.

There was a cyclone of rustling sounds as every man around her pulled out his wallet, striving to be the one to buy that drink for her.

Then, a rich, deep voice sounded from just behind me. "Put 'em away, boys. I got this one."

I inched to the side as a figure pushed past me, nudging me slightly with his arm. For a second, I thought about challenging him. Right up until I saw just how fucking huge the guy was.

I peered around his broad-shouldered form to see Eleanor's reaction. She glanced at him as he approached, her expression barely changing. Just a slight raise of one eyebrow, and an upward curl in the corner of her mouth.

He took the stool beside her, his body moving with athletic grace. Eleanor said something to him, but I was too far away to hear. His reply transformed her face from neutral to vivacious, and it got my insides all whirling and spiking.

It was only as he handed over the money to the barman that I noticed his skin. It was a rich, deep brown, with a slight red tinge.

I bit down on my tongue, desperately wanting to charge over there and reclaim my woman. I even went so far as to pull my wedding band out of my pocket and put it back on.

Something the man said must have resonated with my wife. Her face lit up with laughter, and I was reminded just how beautiful she'd always been. It was tough to remember the last time I'd seen her so alive.

The guy leaned over and whispered straight into Eleanor's ear, and she turned her face to the side. My side. I have no idea what the dude said, but my wife's mouth opened slightly, like she'd gasped with surprise. Then she pursed her lips, like she did when a little moan came out.

When she let her eyes drift closed, I squeezed my whiskey tumbler so hard I thought it might shatter in my hand.

Not only did that man have his mouth right up against my wife's skin, but he was putting all kinds of wicked ideas in her head. My loyal, dedicated, vanilla little wife didn't need to hear all the filthy debauched smut that guy must have been saying.

So why the hell hadn't she slapped him, yet? Why was there a delightful pink flush to her cheeks?

Why the fuck did she have her hand on his arm? And where was her wedding band?

I closed my eyes, trying to center my thoughts. I had to go over there, let her know she was busted. The thought of how her face would change actually got me a little hard.

The widening of her eyes, the pretty little *O* of her mouth. Then the apologies and what-not. I could really score something big out of this. It'd been ages since she'd blown me.

I strode over there and stood behind the guy. The guy with his big, dark hand squeezing my wife's tender thigh.

Yep, I definitely needed to step in. Before she made a big mistake.

A *very* big mistake, I thought, as the guy stood. All six-foot-something-ridiculous of him. I mean, I'm no shrimp, but this guy was in a league of his own.

I'd been sitting when he'd pushed past me before, but even now I was standing, he was still towering above me.

Despite that, I was filled with the power of righteous indignation, and I gave him the polite-coughing of his life.

The guy looked vaguely over his shoulder, not far enough to see me properly. He seemed to simply register that I was no threat to him, then shrugged and returned his attention to Eleanor.

"Excuse me?" I said, and tapped his shoulder. And then I made my killer move, stepping out from behind him, so my wife could see she'd been caught cheating, and the fawning pleas for forgiveness could begin.

Only, she was facing the other way, checking her makeup in the mirror wall behind the bar.

"What's up, buddy?" the big guy said. "Can't you see I'm in conference with this ravishing young lady?"

His voice was deep and smooth, with more than a hint of threat in it. Like his fancy suit and impeccable hair were masking a talent for causing harm. Probably of the *grievous bodily* kind.

"Uh, yeah," I said, noticing the warble in my own voice. "That's what I need to talk to you about."

I switched my attention to my wife's back. All cream-skinned and lightly tanned. How had I lost sight of how fucking gorgeous she was?

"Eleanor?"

"Yes, Douglas? You finally crawled out of your hole, did you?"

"W–what?" Right about now was when she was meant to be shrieking in shock that I'd found her out. But she wasn't even mildly surprised to see me.

"I wondered how long it would take for you to pluck up the courage." She spun slowly on her bar stool until she faced me.

God, up close she was even more perfect. It wasn't the makeup and the hair and the classy-but-slutty dress. Those were wonderful and new, but it was something else. An intangible change in her bearing that made her so damn irresistible.

"You two know each other?" The big man didn't take a backward step. If anything, he eased himself that little bit closer to my wife. "Elle?" he said, directly to her.

"Elle? That's what you're calling yourself tonight?"

She leaned back against the bar, her pert breasts seeming

to swell in her tiny dress. She turned to the big man with a warm smile. "This is my husband, who's here to be unfaithful to me yet again. Isn't that right...*Armand?*"

Oh, fuck. I was completely and utterly fucked. Without lube. Somehow, my secret name had gotten back to my wife. I closed my eyes and mentally waved goodbye to the last little clod of high ground as it crumbled out from under me.

"I, uh...can explain," I said, in the time-honored tradition of men caught cheating. I probably would have followed up with *it's not what it looks like,* but Eleanor cut me off.

"I don't need you to explain, Doug. I just need you to fuck off so Ambrose here can treat me like a lady."

The huge black man angled himself so he was between us, and eased his huge arm over her shoulder. "Like a lady?" he asked her.

"Well, right up until you tear my clothes off and treat me like your dirty little whore."

"Mm. I love the sound of that, Elle."

I reached for Eleanor's hand, to drag her from the stool and back to our house. Walking all the way if need be.

Before I made contact, though, Ambrose pressed his hand to my chest. There was nothing overtly menacing or forceful about it, but I could feel the strength he held in check. "You really oughta respect the lady's wishes, buddy."

He gave me the lightest little shove, and I stumbled a couple of steps back. He reached into his pocket and pulled out a twenty, tossing it toward me. "Here, get yourself a couple drinks on me, buddy. We got things to do."

Even if I'd wanted the money, I wouldn't have been able to catch it. I couldn't stop my hands from clenching into fists.

Don't get me wrong. I'm no hero, and I don't have a death wish. I had no intention of throwing a punch. It was just pure frustration running through me.

I stared, apoplectic, as Eleanor glided off the stool and linked her arm through Ambrose's. They sauntered toward the front door like they'd been together for years.

Of course, I followed them. I wasn't going to take this lying down. Though perhaps Eleanor planned to.

Fuck. Don't even think about that.

"Eleanor, please? We can work this out."

"Oh, you mean like the counselling I've been asking for? *Now* you can find time for that?"

"Please. Come home."

"Home?" she said, barely turning her head toward me. "Oh, you mean that shitty little apartment where I've spent countless evenings waiting for you to pull your shriveled dick out of your latest strumpet, wipe it off with her dress and then grace me with whatever energy you have left?"

Holy hell. "Have...you been following me?"

She simply shook her head. I couldn't see her face properly, but I had no doubt she rolled her eyes as well.

Still, she and Ambrose kept walking away, up the street. And still, I kept following, feeling like a tiresome puppy, yapping at their heels.

"C'mon, Eleanor...don't do this to me?"

She whirled on the spot, her face a mask of disdain. Before she could speak, though, Ambrose interceded.

"Look, Doug—or Armand, if you prefer—you got no play here. Y'understand?"

"No, I don't."

He eased his arm free of Eleanor's and stepped forward. I jumped as he reached his big hands toward me, and only slightly relaxed when I realized he was adjusting my tie. Somehow, that smacked of pure condescension.

"I've known Elle for a few months now." He must have caught the surprised look on my face. "I see she didn't tell you, but then, she never mentioned you to me, either. I wonder why…" His smirk told me he knew exactly why. As did I.

I bit into my tongue, as much to punish myself as to keep from saying something stupid. Because only stupid things were running through my head at that moment.

Ambrose moved his hands down to my lapels and straightened them. "See, I know people. That's my thing. And my guess is, she's done with your shit. I think Elle wants more out of life, and that's where I come in."

"What are you…planning?"

He gave my cheek a light slap. "Oh, I'm planning to wreck this gorgeous wife of yours for all other men. Especially you, buddy."

Suddenly, it all came washing down on me. Understanding, empathy, guilt. A hot shower of cold logic. I'd always known in the back of my mind that I was being a complete prick to Eleanor. Somehow, though, getting away with it that first time had made me think I could get away with it forever.

I shoved my hands in my pockets as I scanned my shoes in shame. "You're right. You're both right. But I can change."

Ambrose slapped his hands down on my shoulders, crisp and hard. "Cool story, bro." Then he simply turned and linked arms with Eleanor again, and they resumed walking away from me.

For a minute or two I followed in silence, not knowing where they were headed. Every block we walked, Ambrose moved his hand lower and lower, until he was cupping my wife's immaculate ass.

And holy fuck…the sight of that hit me like a ton of porn.

Seeing Eleanor all dressed up had reminded me how attractive she'd always been. But now, seeing the lust she inspired in other men…well, that took root inside me. And *outside* of me, if the tingling in my cock was anything to go by.

A block later, they deviated off the sidewalk and up into the front garden of a luxury townhouse. Eleanor glanced back over her shoulder as they reached the door, and seemed surprised to see me still with them.

"Why don't you get along, little Dougie?" Her voice was pure scorn, but even when she belittled me, even with that sneer on her perfect mouth, it still just made me hotter than ever.

What the fuck was going on with me?

Ambrose surprised me then. He rested his huge hand on the back of Eleanor's neck. Maybe it was just to calm her, or maybe he was marking his territory.

"I think your boy should come in. Y'never know…he might learn something."

I was certain my wife would refuse. Send me scuttling home with my tail between my legs. But she surprised me even more than Ambrose had.

"Fine. You wanna come in, Doug? Watch me give Ambrose the best head he's ever had? Watch as I take his magnificent cock every which way a woman can? Be my guest."

Every pore of my skin tingled with shame, sweat…and lust. I closed my eyes as I pictured exactly what my wife just described, and my cock threatened to punch through my pants.

"Last chance, buddy," Ambrose said as he held the door half-closed. I hadn't even heard them open up and walk in.

I scurried as fast as my hard-on would let me, into the plush, dimly-lit interior of Ambrose's townhouse. Everything I walked past gave off expensive and classy vibes, but I only had eyes for my wife.

I followed them both into the living area, and Ambrose stopped me with an outstretched hand.

"You stay there in the hallway, buddy. This here is *our* domain."

There was no fight left in me. All I wanted was to see my wife get fucked hard by this man. A sentence I would never even have thought existed before it flashed through my head.

I nodded and sat on the plush carpet, while Ambrose prowled over to Eleanor.

My wife closed her eyes as the huge black man stalked around her. His mere presence seemed to be both an enormous threat, and an irresistible temptation.

Eleanor's whole body quivered with every breath as Ambrose circled her, like a hunter wearing down his prey. When he glanced his big hand across her shoulder, she jumped and gasped, and it sent fierce signals of want straight down my spine.

My wife's cheeks had gone right through pink and were now a rich, fiery red. Only seeing her like that could remind me how I once inspired such a sense of desire in her.

"Please, Ambrose…touch me?"

The big man came to a halt behind her, his tall, broad frame dwarfing her deliciously curvy body. He glided his hands up from the points of Eleanor's shoulders, to her neck, and the quiver in her legs became a full-blooded tremble.

When he speared his thick fingers into her raven hair, she sucked in a sharp breath so sweet I could almost taste her. I wished I could bottle the look of surrender on her face.

Slowly, Ambrose came down and pressed his lips to the softness of my wife's cheek. He flashed his eyes at me, reminding me of my place, and even that worked dark magic.

I'd never been this hard for Eleanor before. Nor for any of the one-nighters I'd been whoring it up with.

Seeing my wife struggling to keep herself in control,

seeing the potent depth of her arousal...well, that was a show I'd even pay good money for.

Ambrose made a fist in Eleanor's hair, pulling down firmly enough that she slammed back against his chest, her face turned to the ceiling and baring her delicate throat. Every breath she struggled to take made the delicate muscles move in a decidedly erotic ballet beneath her tender skin.

The strap of her little black dress slid down her arm, leaving her naked from shoulder to ear, and with a whole lot of her pert, perfect breast straining to burst free. Seeing all that glorious pale skin, remembering how soft she was, brought a quiet moan of desire from deep inside me.

The big, dark man put his hand on my wife's hip, and slid it gradually upward. The moment he cupped her breast, he planted his open mouth against her creamy throat, and Eleanor had to catch her breath.

My cock was so damn hard it ached. It was a torture, but the most beautiful torture I'd ever known. I ground my palm against it through my pants, closing my eyes and savoring the sharp tingles of pleasure.

For a few moments, I simply focused on myself. On my own desires. And then remembered how that was all I'd been doing for the last year or so.

When I returned my focus to my wife and her lover, I was pleasantly surprised to see Ambrose had stripped Eleanor down to nothing but her panties and stockings. Her gorgeous bare breasts quivered and heaved with the deep breaths she took, as her dark-skinned man nipped at the skin of her shoulder.

The sweet contrast of Ambrose's huge dark hands on my wife's alabaster belly was like visual poetry. Every move the man made had the essence of a dancer. Smooth, graceful, and with a clear purpose.

In this case, the purpose was to get my wife naked and fill

her with his cock. Even so, I was totally mesmerized by the process.

Ambrose bent down and scooped Eleanor into his arms like she was a tiny puppy. He strode easily across the room and placed her on her back across the table.

He gripped her flimsy black panties in his hand and simply tore them off her, as easy as plucking a petal from a flower. Eleanor made a tiny squealing sound in reaction, and even that had my belly tightening, rolling, tingling with want.

Ambrose dropped to his knees and tugged Eleanor toward himself, her skin gliding across the polished table top. He stopped only when her sweet, bare pussy crashed against his mouth.

I watched, transfixed, as this huge black man gorged himself on the glistening tender flesh of my wife's most intimate place. His deep voice became a coarse growl as he savored Eleanor; her sweet, musky flavor and her spicy scent.

Even from my place in the hallway, I swore I caught traces of her arousal in the air. It just made me hungrier than ever.

"Damn, Elle," the big man murmured, barely taking his mouth off her delicious cunt. "Your pussy is fucking perfect."

My wife arched her back with pleasure, and it reminded me it had been months since I'd complimented her in any way. And even longer since I'd gone down on her.

She reached between her slender thighs and hooked her hands around the back of Ambrose's head, pulling him against herself. The wanton little strumpet. God, it made me hot to see her taking what she wanted.

Ambrose drove one thick finger inside her pussy as he sucked on her clit, and in seconds, my beautiful, naked wife became a shrieking, shameless, thrashing creature of pure ecstasy.

It hit me like a gunshot that I'd never made her come like that. Not once. Oh, I'd got her off plenty of times, but now I could see, those had all been some variation of Orgasm Lite.

As she gradually came down from her personal heaven, I suddenly understood just how much sexual pleasure my wife had, pulsing around inside her. I'd been too much of a prick to even *think* about that, let alone explore it.

Ambrose nipped her inner thigh and stood, removing his jacket and shirt to reveal a body as beautiful as it was dark.

Broad and tall, toned by the gym and decorated with tribal tattoo art. The man was my complete opposite in almost every way.

Eleanor rolled herself up into a seated position and put her hands around the man's bull neck. She slid them down and around, exploring every inch of the man's skin.

I gasped as she leaned forward and took his thick nipple into her mouth. And I groaned as she worked his belt and pants open.

When she dug her hands down inside his underwear, I lost the power of thought. Forgot how to breathe, even.

With her hands getting busy, Eleanor paused and looked up into Ambrose's eyes. Her expression was one of disbelief, and I had a sneaking suspicion I knew why.

Then, when she pushed his pants and boxers down, I knew I was right.

Ambrose's mighty cock sprang free of his underwear, like a bear pouncing on my wife.

"Oh, my god," Eleanor moaned. "Oh, my fucking god."

She took the words right out of my mouth. And then took that big, black cock in hers.

Eleanor bent down and slid Ambrose's broad head

between her lips, cupping his fat balls and driving herself halfway down that monster before she had to stop.

Of all the things I'd seen tonight, that was absolutely the hottest. So far, at least. For all kinds of reasons, Eleanor hadn't sucked my cock in ages. I'd almost forgotten how fucking good she was at it. And I'd never known she could take that much meat in her mouth.

Slowly, my wife pumped Ambrose's cock in and out. Without skipping a beat, without releasing him for even a second, she glided off the table and onto her knees.

Ambrose took a fistful of her lush, dark hair and pulled, and Eleanor whimpered with clear desire around the meaty treat in her mouth.

Deeper and deeper she took him, clawing at the man's ass to pull him closer. The sheer hunger she had for that thick, dark cock was an absolute revelation to me.

I couldn't take my eyes off my wife. Seeing the way Eleanor blossomed at Ambrose's touch, at his words, made me understand her just that little bit better.

And seeing what a horny little thing she could be had my cock straining for release. I'd always known Douglas Junior had a mind of its own. Now, it was like it knew what it was missing. Pressing against my pants like a cry for attention.

I unzipped and pulled it out, squeezing it hard in my fist. The thing was so sensitive, it felt as if it had a hair trigger. No way was I going to mess this up by coming early, though.

Eleanor let Ambrose slip from her mouth with a sticky, sucking sound. The huge man simply lifted her from the floor and kissed her deeply, filling her mouth again. This time with his tongue.

My wife moaned with pleasure as her entire body seemed to turn to liquid in his hands. He grabbed her tight ass and squeezed, as she curled her gorgeous stockinged legs around his waist.

When she tightened her body's grip on him, Ambrose groaned and arched, letting his head fall back. He was like a wolf howling. He was the king of beasts and the apex predator.

He brought his face back down level with Eleanor's, his top lip curled into a cruel and hungry smile.

"I been wantin' to fuck you since the moment I saw you, Elle."

"So fucking do it, Ambrose. I'm so wet for you. I want your huge, black cock in my cunt."

A wave of shameful arousal washed through my body. Eleanor had never spoken like that to me. I'd never even heard her say *cunt* before. The shock of it was as hot as the sound of her need.

Ambrose parked my wife's perfect ass on the table, her arms and legs still wrapped around him. He took a fistful of her hair and tightened it against her scalp, as he reached between their bodies to slot his cock in place.

They paused for a moment, Eleanor's eyes wide with anticipation. And probably a little fear. That fucking cock of his was so damn big.

But this man had clearly awoken something inside her. A spirit of adventure, a well of desire. Eleanor angled her head up to bite into Ambrose's bottom lip, with a little snarling sound. Without words, she'd told him exactly what she wanted.

And I couldn't believe how much I wanted it, too.

The huge, black man growled out his desire straight into my wife's mouth, devouring her tongue as he gripped her hair and hip.

And with a sharp, punching drive of his hips, Ambrose thrust his long, thick cock deep inside my wife.

It was Eleanor's turn to howl at the moon, though she did

it without sound. Without voice. It was as if Ambrose's magic wand had cast a spell of silence on her.

She simply gripped him tighter, pulling at his ass with her feet, scratching her nails across his back, hard enough to maybe draw blood.

Ambrose took the skin of her throat between his teeth and growled with need, gradually lowering Eleanor's body to the table.

After a moment, her mind seemed to come down from whatever new dimension she'd been transported to. Ambrose stood tall between her wide-spread legs, gliding himself almost all the way out of her, and my wife gripped his arms as if afraid he was done with her.

I couldn't resist looking down at his monster cock. All glistening with my wife's juices, it looked even darker than before. And bigger.

Eleanor sank her nails deep into Ambrose's forearms, creasing her brow with frustration.

"Oh, god, Ambrose. I can't wait any longer. Fuck me, fuck me, *fuck me*."

He curled his top lip up as he narrowed his eyes. He looked like a heavyweight boxer who'd just taken a surprise punch...and was ready to return fire.

I held my breath—and gripped my cock—as he widened his stance. Suddenly, he burst into action, thrusting himself in and out of Eleanor's beautiful cunt, grinding like an engine.

Every blow of his hips washed through her body like the tide, her juicy tits dancing on her chest like teenagers at a rave.

I pumped my hand in rhythm, firing off bursts of ecstasy deep within me. The sparks and bolts of bliss seemed to come from somewhere so dark, I hadn't known it was there. And they fired through into new places I'd never imagined.

Eleanor arched her back off the table, presenting her tits to the gods. Ambrose gripped those soft, fleshy mounds and squeezed, thumbing her nipples as he pistoned his massive cock in and out.

"Oh, fuck…Ambrose…I'm gonna…"

She opened her mouth in a wide O shape, her breath rushing in and out as she struggled to keep up with what must have been a hurricane of bliss inside her.

Ambrose's hands turned to claws as he tightened his grip on my wife's breasts, and he arched backward to roar at the stars.

I squeezed my cock harder as I pumped like a demon, my own climax coming over me so fast it was like an ambush.

With a strangled moan, I finished myself off, squirting my hot juice out and catching it in my palm, just as my wife and her new lover writhed in harmony with their own climaxes.

As my orgasm faded, my body turned soft. I arched forward, sitting on my feet, like a wizened old gnome. And I had no doubt shame was the cause.

Shame at how much of an asshole I'd been to Eleanor. Shame that while I'd *chosen* to seek sex with strangers, my inattention to her needs had basically *forced* her to.

And especially, a dark but delicious shame for having loved so much the sight of my wife getting roughed up and fucked by the most magnificent man I'd ever seen.

The craziest part of it all, though, was the sharp streak of want, of need, or pure desire, that curled around my shame, like a python. Squeezing it into a tight, hard column, melding it with the very essence of me.

Only when my head cleared did I register that Ambrose still had his huge cock buried deep in my wife's pussy. He'd shot his load inside her.

Fresh tingles of pleasurable shame rose on the back of my neck. That was the one thing I'd never done with Eleanor.

Finished inside her. Even when she begged me to, I'd held back. Like it was a fucking power trip for me.

The knowledge that she'd just willingly taken Ambrose's cum simply blew my mind. Just the thought she might be growing another man's baby inside her added fresh kindling to the fire of shameful desire inside me.

Eleanor finally managed to catch her breath, and she turned to look straight at me. Her face was more relaxed, and it seemed a lot of her anger had evaporated.

"How did that feel, Douglas?"

The tone of her voice told me she'd started this with the simple desire to get back at me. That this was supposed to be a lesson on fucking with someone else's affections.

But there was also a tiny lilt of hope in there. It was weird to me that I'd never noticed the nuances of my wife's speech until now.

"That felt...god, I don't know if I have the words."

"Try," she hummed, her face going slack with bliss as Ambrose glided his cock out of her.

"I...I hated it. I hated it because I...oh, god, I fucking loved it."

Eleanor rolled onto her side, accentuating the delightful hills and valleys of her body. "Where do you see us going, Doug? Can you stop fucking other women?"

Just the fact she used the short version of my name told me there was hope for me. For us.

"I can," I said, my voice low. "But I'm hoping..."

"Yes?"

"I want you, honey. I never want to lose you. But...I want what we had tonight." I swept my hand around, indicating her, and Ambrose, and the whole place.

"Meaning?"

I swallowed the last shred of doubt. "I want to watch you

fuck other men. Not just Ambrose. Anyone you want. Two at a time. A gang-bang. Whatever turns you on."

Eleanor pursed her lips and drew in a breath that sounded almost like a moan. Seeing the pink in her cheeks growing darker, I continued, "Because I now know, whatever turns you on...turns *me* on just as much."

THE END
Get Access to over 20 more FREE Erotica Downloads at Shameless Book Deals

Shameless Book Deals is a website that shamelessly brings you the very best erotica at the best prices from the best authors to your inbox every day. Sign up to our newsletter to get access to the daily deals and the Shameless Free Story Archive!

CUCKED BY THE BLACK BOSS BY ELIZA DEGAULLE

Jessie and Mitchel are newlyweds, and they're relying on Mitchel getting a promotion at his job to secure their future. Just as soon as he starts to make the appeal though, Mitchel blows everything in front of his black boss, Devon. With Mitch drunk and useless, it's on Jessie to make things happen and keep her man's job. Devon will give her what she wants and more, but he wants something in return. For her to take him, raw and unprotected. If Mitch is watching as it happens? So be it.

$\sim$

I've always striven to be the most supportive wife I could be.

Like how I spent the last four hours sweating over a hot stove, making brownies, potato salad, my grandmother's famed baked beans, and some vegan mac & cheese.

I personally wasn't a vegan, but Mitch insisted that bringing something that fit those restrictions would ring well with his boss and the staff. Like it would show that he considered others or something like that, as he put it.

"We need to make ourselves look like a nuclear family, Jessie. Like we're people that can be relied on for the long haul. That's what Devon is looking for in his new Executive Vice President."

"Sure, sure," I said, walking along, being careful not to drop the food.

I hadn't met this Devon before. I didn't even know what his last name was. All I knew was that he was Mitchel's boss, and Mitchel talked about him all the time, about how he was the one he needed to appeal to.

This Devon's house though? Fuck it was huge. To be my man's boss, it didn't surprise me that he had such a mansion of a home.

"Are you ready, Jessie? This is important. We need to be on," he said, looking my way with those puppy dog eyes of his.

Mitchel was a sweet and kind man. A good soul. I loved him more than any other, but I wasn't blind to his weaknesses as a person.

His spine was made of jelly.

Like the man had his share of berserk buttons which would get him good and angry, but when it came to facing down his boss? We needed to appease super hard according to him.

We were at that crossroads in our lives. Married for a year and faced with the reality of what we wanted for our future.

Me? I was doing odd jobs. Working in retail, doing some gig economy stuff. Him? A professional with actual forward potential. I didn't grow up dreaming to be a homemaker or whatever, but after putting in years in the retail world, it suddenly seemed a whole lot more tempting.

There was also the idea of a family and if we wanted it. We didn't want to bring a child into the world if the two of us were struggling to get by. So the past few weeks? Mitchel had talked up this opportunity. The old vice president stepped down, and now the slot was open. If he got the job, and the pay raise and benefits that went with it, he'd make more than enough for both of us. We could start a family and I could dedicate myself to being a mother, or some sort of artistic passion, or whatever else.

"Alright, make yourself smile and look happy, Jessie. Remember, you're helping represent me here," Mitchel said as he rang the doorbell.

"Don't over think it, Mitch. I'm certain you'll get the job if you don't go and make an absolute fool of yourself."

"Yeah, well, that's what I'm worried about."

The door opened, and a man appeared.

I was immediately taken aback by his presence.

No, he wasn't horribly deformed or maimed or anything like that. It was definitely the opposite.

He was a big, and quite imposing, black man.

It definitely wasn't what I thought of when I pictured Mitchel's boss in my head. Not a six-and-half-foot-tall slab of meat.

He towered over Mitch, making my husband's intimidation a little bit more understandable.

"Ah, Mitch, ya made it my man."

Mitch nodded.

"And who is this lovely angel you have with you?" He smiled my way, and I was frozen in place, being as anxious as Mitchel was, but for likely an entirely different reason. "A virgin sacrifice to help you get your promotion, eh?"

"What?" Mitchel snapped. He shook his head. "No, no, this is my wife. She brought a bunch of treats for the cookout."

"Oh. I guess I'll have to settle for tasting something else of hers then." He smiled my way. "It's not what I would want to taste if I had a choice, but we can't always get what we want, can we?"

Mitchel laughed nervously. He wasn't enjoying his boss's aggressive approach as much as I... um... was.

Yeah, all this talk was making me smile. It should have been something I wrote off as inappropriate and crass, something that I should be telling my husband to be filing some sort of sexual harassment claim about.

Instead, I was entertaining the thoughts of infidelity with this man I barely knew. To say I was feeling shame with myself would be an understatement.

"Come on in, don't just sit in the doorway," he said, waving us in.

We obeyed his command and walked to the table in the back. There were dozens of people throughout the backyard, some wandering the house saying their greetings to Mitchel.

I put down the dishes I had brought, hoping they'd be good enough to get Mitchel the job he wanted. He did seem friendly with his boss, so that was likely a good sign.

"So, does your wife have a name? Or should I just refer to her as *your wife*?" he said with a smirk.

I spoke up first. "Jessie," I said. Shakily I offered my hand, and he took it.

His grip was tight, almost crushing. "Jessie, huh? Lovely name. Nice to finally have a name and beautiful face to put to Mitch's rambling. The man talks about you all the time, just always calls you his wife."

I blushed, as well as laughed, looking my husband's way. He was absolutely crazy about me, and he still was a year on. I hadn't regretted marrying him yet.

Except for the big black temptation in front of me.

"So what have you got there, beautiful?"

I laid out the dishes, and nervously began to explain. "Uh,

here's some vegan mac and cheese. First time making it so I hope it's okay."

"Lara will love it I'm sure."

"Is Lara your wife?" I said forcing a smile.

"Oh no, she's an employee. Only tells me she's a vegan once a month or so, so she's good by me."

Damn. I could have been calmer if I knew he was married, even if he wasn't the most faithful. I turned back to the food to keep my mind and my eyes off of him. "Uh, these are my grandmother's long-held family recipe for baked beans. It's the only baked beans I really like, and they're really good."

"It ain't a good get-together unless everyone's got horrible gas." Another chuckle. "Not to say a pretty girl like you would do such a thing."

"And... uh... these brownies. And potato salad. Just typical brownies and potato salad. I followed a recipe from a book for the latter, and the first is uh... Betty Crocker?"

"The kids will love them I'm sure. Not everything has to be expertly crafted for people to enjoy them."

"Kids? You have kids?"

Another deep, hearty laugh from this man. "No. Not yet. I was talking about the other employees' kids here. My kids will come I'm sure. Maybe sooner than I realize, you never know."

"Uh huh."

"What, you volunteering to help me with that?"

As I was talking things over with Devon, enduring his relentless flirting, something was happening just out of sight of me.

Fists balling up, teeth grinding, my dear husband? Well he was absolutely pissed.

"Watch it," he said, his tone low and seething.

"Hmm?" Devon replied an eyebrow raised.

"Watch what you're saying to her, Devon. She's my wife, she's not some piece of meat on the market for you to salivate over."

Oh shit.

Devon was probably going a bit far, but Mitch suddenly growing a spine? Yeah, this wasn't the best time to do it. The look the boss was giving in response though?

He wasn't exactly pleased. No, he looked very much hostile to Mitchel's words.

I expected him to turn that booming voice of his to anger. Shout Mitch down, tell him he's fired, and put our plans for the future really on the back burner. We'd go from looking to starting a family to struggling to survive in no time flat.

Luckily, Devon's anger faded away, and he just smiled in Mitchel's direction. "Why don't you stick around until after the party, Mitch? We'll have a nice long discussion about your future in the company."

He reached over, patted my husband on the back.

It did little to ease him as Devon turned and walked away from the two of us.

Mitchel immediately collapsed like a house of cards as soon as his boss was out of sight. "Oh shit, I shouldn't have said that. I shouldn't have been so..."

I let out a sigh. He was falling apart, so it was on me to keep everything together. "Just... calm down, Mitch. Just go apologize. Explain yourself. He seems like a reasonable man. It was your love for your wife that made you lash out."

"Oh I know, I know," he murmured. His eyes weren't on mine. They were instead searching the room.

They swiftly found what he was looking for.

"I need a drink. Badly."

"Mitchel, is the best time to be drinking?"

"I need the liquid courage to face Devon again, Jessie! I can't just go in stone cold sober."

A long sigh escaped my lips. I couldn't stop the man from this. Maybe it would help him. Maybe it would calm him down and do as he said – give him the courage to stand up to his boss.

Knowing Mitchel? It was unlikely, but right now, it wasn't like I had many other options.

~

"Jes... jes one more. And that'll be enough."

It had been just one more for the past twelve.

With all he drank, I was now more worried about alcohol poisoning than him being fired.

"Not one more. Just... take a nap here, Mitch. You can barely walk," I said, slapping the cushion.

"Oh... you wanna go and do... the things? Right here? You dirty girl you."

He moved to kiss me. It would have been sweet if he wasn't so drunk that he was trying to kiss the air a foot to the right of my face. With his miss, he planted himself face first in the cushions. He was so very slow to turn himself over.

The company cookout had started to clear out hours ago. A few hangers on stayed behind to talk, but what was dozens of people before were now few enough to be counted on one hand.

As soon as some old guy took off, it'd only be Mitch, myself, and... well..

Devon.

The conversation the two were having was very much animated. Unlike what was talked about earlier, Devon was in good spirits with this man.

Usually, that would be a good omen. Seeing how easily he stifled his hostility earlier though? It didn't really mean much.

Especially with his employee one beer away from blackout drunk. Whatever he looked like right now, it sure as hell wasn't an Executive Vice President.

Right now, I was worried about getting Mitch through the night with just his job intact, not so much the promotion. I had accepted that was long gone when Mitch started on his second six-pack.

The old man was leaving, and soon, Devon was alone again. He was doing some minor cleaning, and then he would be heading straight for us.

He would see what a wreck Mitch was, and then he would fire him.

"Jes... get me another, and I'll be fine... don't cut me off now, babe..." He was reaching out into nothing, grabbing for what I assumed he thought was my hand.

I took a deep breath myself. I wasn't just going to sit here and let my life go to hell. If Mitch couldn't explain himself, then I would explain Mitch. Tell him what a good worker he is, how he's so stressed, and how much he loves me. How that leads to him being a bit protective of me at times.

Midnight, the clock on the wall said. Maybe he was tired himself, and would be more open to showing mercy with the right words?

Hypotheticals wouldn't help me.

I needed to act, and I needed to act now.

Helping my nearly unconscious husband to sit down properly, I was almost pleased that he was now just dozing off. Sleeping, he couldn't do any more damage than he did.

It was my turn to contemplate drinking for courage. Even as my husband drowned himself, I'd only taken in about half of a single bottle.

No. I needed my head straight. Show that my man had a good woman behind him, someone who was willing to help him succeed. That should definitely count for something.

I made my way over to him. He was quick to perk up as I approached.

"Ah, Jessie. How've you been enjoying the night?"

"Not as much as I should I admit," I said. "Look, I'm here to talk for Mitch. He's a bit..."

"Oh, we're doing business then?" he interrupted.

"I guess we are?"

"Then we're going to my office."

"Uh. Kay. I'm assuming that means a home office."

"As much as I'd like to ride alone in a car with you, Jessie, yes, I mean home office. Come."

With a tinge of fear, I followed Devon up the stairs and into a room.

The first thing I saw when I entered?

A king-sized bed.

My eyes went wide as my mind quickly jumped to a very filthy conclusion.

One more step inside, and I saw the desk, complete with executive's chair and closed laptop. He walked around the desk, sat in the chair, kicked his feet up on it, giving me a sight of those tree trunkish legs of his.

"Um, I'm not trying to offend or question you, but why do you have a bed in your office? This house seems big enough to have a separate room for that."

"Hey, I like being comfortable. Besides, I do some of my best work in a bed."

I walked right into that.

"Listen, I want to apologize for what happened earlier."

"With your husband snapping at me?"

I nodded. "Mitch is a very easygoing man. He doesn't let much get to him, just only when it comes to me. You may have only been flirting for fun, but to him, he thought you were harassing me."

"Jessie, my girl, don't you worry about that. I was messing

with him back. I was actually impressed that he had a spine after all."

"What, you liked him snapping at you?"

"Your man is a bit of a pushover. Sweet, hardworking, thinks of others, but he lacks that man aspect. How he earned a woman like you I'll never know."

I let out a sigh. "So you're not going to fire him."

Another laugh from Devon, him shaking his head. "I wasn't. Not for that no. But then I saw the mess he became."

I gritted my teeth again, knowing exactly what he was talking about.

"How can I rely on a man who gets pissing himself drunk at the sight of the most minor adversity? The kind of man who sends his woman to do his business for him."

"Mitchel didn't send me, I'm here on my own accord."

"Yeah, well, it seems pretty clear to me that it's because he can't even walk right now. I'm sorry, but I really think I'm going to have to let him go. He's too risky if he's that volatile."

All too quickly I snapped back at him. "You can't do that! Don't do that!"

"Or what? I'm allowed to fire people if they give me good reason to. Being an overly emotional drunk is a solid reason for dismissal."

"He needs this job, Devon. We need this job. We're relying on it for our future."

"I need reliable employees, Jessie. How can I trust that Mitch will be reliable?"

"Because he is. Because I'm there to keep him straight."

"You? I'm hiring Mitch, though, not you."

I grunted in frustration. "He told me he wanted me to come to this company cookout because showing you that he was a family man would be important to you. He is a family man. He wants to start a family, but he isn't reckless enough to do it unemployed."

"And I'm presuming this is important to you as well?"

"Well, yeah, I'm the one he wants to start the family with!"

He laughed. "Nice and eager. That man is lucky to have you. Maybe we can negotiate something, Jessie."

"Negotiate?" I didn't like the way that he said that word.

"I could see a damn good reason to keep Mitch on board if he could offer me something that no one else could. Say, like a certain pretty ass white girl if you know what I mean."

For a time, I stared at him. Silent, and my eyes wide, I was struggling to believe what I was hearing.

If Mitch heard this, he would have freaked out again. Mitch wasn't here though. He was downstairs unconscious, and making me worried he wasn't going to choke on his own vomit.

"Keep him on. Maybe still give him that Executive Vice President he's after. I mean, a pretty ass white girl like you representing him? Willing to do anything to get what her man wants? How could anyone turn down an offer like that?"

I swallowed, and closed my eyes. A million thoughts were crossing my mind.

One train of thought? How dare this man. Where does he get off? Another boss mad with power, throwing it around to get what he wants.

The other, though?

It dreamed of being bad. Indulging. Seeing what this behemoth of a man could do to me. He had no lack of confidence, and it'd be interesting to see what that meant if I allowed him to do his other sort of business in this room.

He took his feet off the desk and stood tall again, walking my way and stopping just to tower over me and make me feel so very small.

"Let me take good care of you, Jessie. Let me show what you've been missing if you only ever have fucked guys like Mitch."

"He's my husband," I said. "I love him."

"Oh, I know. You wouldn't be here in front of me if you didn't. But you want to help him. You got something I want, baby. I say we got a pretty obvious deal in front of us."

I stayed quiet. I didn't want to answer, because quite honestly I was terrified of what that answer would be.

"Oh, I get it. You're not sure what you want your answer to be. That's fine. Let's ease you into it then."

"What do you mean by that?"

He leaned back on his desk, eyeing me up and down. "Why don't you slip off that shirt of yours for me? Maybe I'll be satisfied with just seeing a little more of the pretty ass white girl."

That didn't seem likely. Yet did I really have a choice in the matter? I didn't want to deal with the anxiety of Mitchel losing his job. Especially if word got out that he was fired for drinking of all things. Nuance didn't matter on first impressions.

A deep sigh, and I stepped back from Devon. I reached for the hem of my shirt, and started to hike it up. I wasn't in anything fancy. Just a t-shirt and some shorts. It was a cook-out, not a banquet after all.

This all made me feel like I should have worn a whole lot more though.

My shirt was tossed to the ground, and I felt his eyes rain down on me and my now suddenly inadequate feeling bra.

There was something oddly exciting about the situation. Of having him look my way, up and down my body. It felt so damn wrong. I was a married woman. I barely knew the man in front of me.

Yet it felt like the good kind of wrong. Like I was a sinner, like I was the bad girl.

Pretty ass white girl? I wasn't one to brag, but I lived the stereotype. Never got in trouble. Never caused my parents any headaches.

Never cheated on a boyfriend, and definitely never cheated on my husband.

Right then, though?

It made me feel sexy. Exotic. Like I was one of those bad girl femme fatales that they made movies about.

"Keep going. I'm liking what I'm seeing, baby. Can see why your man would get into a fight over you."

More blushing. Shorts. I was wearing underwear underneath, so it wasn't like taking off my shorts would reveal anything more. I kicked them off, as well as my shoes and socks. Not because I thought he had a foot fetish or anything, but because standing there in my underwear with them on? It made an awkward situation even more awkward.

He just smiled. He wanted more. PG-13 wasn't going to cut it for someone like him.

I'd have to go R. Probably NC-17 and veer off into X before I was all done with him.

Unhooking my bra, I summoned the courage to drop it. I could just claim to be European where being topless wasn't a big deal.

Yeah. He'd believe that. So would Mitch, who knew I was born and raised in Bumfuck, Nowhere, USA.

Whatever. I dropped the bra. This man got to see my tits. I shouldn't have been too bothered by the idea.

I shouldn't have been so aroused by the idea.

"Nice and perky looking," he said. "Can't wait to get a feel of them to see if they're as luscious as they appear."

More blushing from me.

He stood up from his lean, approaching me, and wrapping those dark arms around my hips. I still had my panties on, but the way he was looking at me? He didn't care. He saw a beautiful woman in front of him and he most definitely wanted to indulge in it.

Devon's lips lingered closely to mine, ready to kiss me. I had my head turned, but the temptation to give in was so strong.

This was wrong. This was so, so wrong. I should have pushed him away. I should have run. Money wasn't worth my morals.

However...

It wasn't like Mitch had to know.

Just... do this. He was out like a light downstairs, and he'd be sleeping for hours. I'd probably have to wait until he woke up even, because there was no way I was going to be able to carry him.

He wouldn't know. It would be my little secret. Something only I knew. I'd never tell him, and he'd never find out.

Unless Devon told him.

No. He wouldn't. My gut was telling me that Devon looked at Mitch as a good employee, regardless of what he said.

He just wanted me much more than he wanted Mitch to keep working for him.

What if, though, I got pregnant?

I trembled at the thought. No. This man was single and rich. That wouldn't happen. He'd use a condom, pull-out, or hell, I wouldn't have been surprised if he already had a vasectomy.

That's what would happen. There's no way he was one of those big black guys who got off on breeding white women?

Was he?

"Are you going to stay there looking pouty and confused? I know you want me, Jessie baby. You're trying to act like you don't, but you're not very good at acting the part."

He wouldn't find out, I repeated to myself. All my

worrying was pointless. I'd do this for him.

I'd do this for myself.

So I turned my face toward him and accepted Devon's kiss.

Full force, full power. All of his lips on mine and showing no restraint in not pushing the situation further. His tongue infiltrated my mouth, and it was less about leading me along as commanding me to entwine myself with him.

I was enraptured in the moment, but reality had a way of yanking you right back.

"What the fuck is this?"

Our kiss broke, and I stumbled away from Devon.

Mitch was right there. His face was red, and I knew that was mostly from being drunk as all hell, but him being incredibly angry? That definitely didn't help things.

"Jessie! What's the meaning of this? You're buck fucking naked, having my boss kiss you like he's about to do a hell of a lot more!"

"Mitch, I... uh... I'm not naked..."

"You might as well be!"

What the hell did I think that would prove? That I thought it was okay to kiss another man if I kept my panties on?

Mitch was glaring my way. The rage was fading, and it was being replaced by sadness quite quickly.

I had betrayed him.

"Jessie... what... what are you..." His words still slurred. Anger could only sober him up so much. "What are you doing?"

At that moment it felt like a knife had plunged into my heart. That I was the worst woman on the entire planet, that I didn't deserve anyone's love or caring touch.

There was someone else in the room besides Mitch and I though.

He had things to say about all this.

"Buck up, kiddo," he said, mockingly toward Mitch. He then grabbed me by the hips again and pulled me close. "She's doing nothing right now that's not for you."

"What are you talking about?"

"Your woman here? She begged me not to fire your ass for the shit you pulled tonight. She was willing to do anything for you to keep your job. She didn't betray you, Mitch. Hardly."

"But... you're, like... holding her like you're about to fuck her."

"She's offering herself to me. For you. Since you're such a failure, you should be happy you have such a damn fine woman holding you up like this."

"Is this true, Jessie?"

We hadn't formally agreed to that, but it became quite clear that Devon, for all of his lecherous ways, had a bit of a heart in that massive frame of his.

I nodded wordlessly. "I wanted to make sure you kept your job."

"There we go," Devon said. "All's understood now."

"What? You're still going to fuck her with me right here?" Mitch said, pulling at his hair.

"Enjoy the show, Mitch. I'm going to show your woman the night of a lifetime. Might ruin you for her, but that's your problem, not mine."

"You can't be serious."

Devon was completely serious, and he showed it by kissing me again. His hand going down my body, taking a grip of my breast, tweaking it, a stinging bit of bliss shooting through it.

This was still wrong. My husband watching another man fondle me like this? That didn't magically make it okay.

He undid the buttons of his shirt, revealing that hairless

chest that was just as ripped and toned as the rest of him would have suggested. It was quite the visual sight.

All while he did this, he continued to kiss me, and damn, he was good at it. As paralyzed by indecision as I was, I couldn't help but get into what he was doing and follow his lead.

Goosebumps popped up all over me as he caressed me, his hands going down to my ass, and getting quite the grip full of those. He picked me up, spun me around and sat me down on his desk.

His kisses then went lower and lower on me, down across my breasts. His beard's rough hair tickled me as he descended, prickling at my areola more as he went.

Without a big black guy blocking my view, I could look over at Mitch. Watch him watch me, and how the situation was unfolding.

His eyes? They were glued on me still. I had thought that he wouldn't be able to bear to look at me as this happened, but it seemed to be the opposite. His eyes were wide in shock, but there was definitely something I recognized beneath that.

Desire. I knew when this man was horny. More than anyone else.

A hand went on my chest, and Devon urged me to lay back. He slid down my body, and with a great burst of strength, tore out the bottom of my panties. I looked at him with surprise, and then he dove between my legs and surprised me even more.

His lips on my clit, I cried out as he began to work me down there. His fingers thrust into my slit and started to fuck me as his tongue continued to do work on my nub.

I wasn't expecting him to eat me out, but I was expecting this pace. This frenzy. This wasn't about romance, this wasn't about him showing how much he loved me.

This was about dominance, and it sure as hell wasn't about dominance over me.

No. I was just the tool who would get to enjoy the performance.

It was about dominance over Mitch.

Devon had the power. Devon was the man. Devon was in control.

Not only financially, but now?

He had his wife beneath him. Eating her out. Making her writhe and moan for him.

God, was he doing that.

I tried not to enjoy it too much at first. Maybe to save Mitch some face.

There was only so much I could do though. It was a relentless sensual assault going my way. From the growing orgasm inside me, to the touch of his hands, to even that brash beard of his rubbing against my thighs. I twisted and turned on that desk, my moans growing louder and more out of control.

He wasn't letting me savor this either. He was all about a relentless, focused assault that would make me squirm, that would make me scream.

The orgasm that was building inside me was coming at me so strong and so quick, that I couldn't contain myself for much longer.

It was all too abrupt when the orgasmic train finally hit me. The electricity shooting all through my body, the epicenter my poor clit. Wave after wave...

Then it kept coming.

He had to have known that I'd come. It was pretty damn clear. He was continuing though. His tongue thrusting in and out of my pussy, his fingers rapidly rubbing my clit. The feeling inside me remained strong, receding only a bit.

Before it came rushing right back at me. Twisting and

turning, my back arching and everything writhing in glorious bliss, all I was was orgasm at that moment.

As the waves crashed upon me again and again, Devon finally relented, leaving me panting and weak before him.

Making me cum once? That wasn't enough for him. That didn't drive the point home of how good he was. No. He needed to make me cum again and again, supposedly something even Mitch wouldn't be able to do.

If he did or didn't, it didn't matter at that moment. I just enjoyed the ache and everything going on. I heard the undoing of a belt, and the sound of it hitting the floor.

He was stripping down. I looked between my legs and saw that mountain of a man there, briefly thought I'd be greeted with a view of him in only boxers.

No.

Devon was a man who got to the point. Those were already gone, unnecessary to what he wanted to accomplish.

So I saw it.

His cock.

Throbbing. Hard. Intimidating.

I wasn't going to say my husband had a micropenis or any hyperbole like that. I thought he was packing something pretty good. It was just that....

A giant pulsing rod of meat in front of me. A tinge of precum at the end of it. Big, heavy balls hanging beneath it.

The whole package was aimed at me, my torn panties, and my very vulnerable sex.

My eyes were wide as I briefly reevaluated the whole logistics of how sex worked.

Briefly, I glanced over at Mitch. He was still watching the scene intently, despite Devon's obvious flaunting of himself over him. I thought he was standing still and straight until I noticed that his hand was moving over the crotch of his pants.

I laughed softly. He was fighting himself not to masturbate in front of all this.

Actually... that sounded kind of hot. Mitch masturbating to me getting fucked. It was an odd idea, but the strange allure of it was undeniable to me.

"Going to fuck your woman now, Mitch," Devon said aloud. "Gonna ruin her for you. She ain't gonna want anything to do with your needle dick after I'm done with her."

That may have been taking it a bit far, but... well... I wasn't going to say anything right now. Especially anything that would stop the oncoming train from plunging into my sex.

"Wait!" Mitch said, rasping, strangely out of breath for someone who was just standing there watching.

"Wait, what, little man?" Devon said looking his way.

"I'll let this happen. I'll let you fuck my wife. But you need to wear a condom."

"A condom?" He laughed at the idea.

"She's off her birth control. I don't want to risk..." If Mitch hadn't brought it up, I would have never said a thing. I was off in la la land, any conscious thought I had left dedicated to psyching myself up to what was to come.

"You don't want to risk what, Mitch?"

"She could get pregnant."

"Is that a problem, Mitch?"

"Uh..."

Devon laughed again. "I think your girl here said you wanted to start a family. The way I see it I think I'm just going to help you along to that."

"But..."

"This is me cutting you a break, Mitch. We're doing things my way, and my way? I ain't wearing no fucking condom."

Mitch tried to come up with some sort of answer, but he didn't say anything else, just gritting his teeth in frustration.

I just looked on. Ready for whatever. I thought about maybe speaking up for myself, but I had already done more than enough.

There was also the fact that I wanted this. I wanted it all. I was a married woman. Would I ever get a chance like this ever again?

Bring it on. Bring on the risks, whatever they may be.

Devon loomed over me, and flashed me another smile. "I'm going to fuck you, Jessie. I'm going to fuck you like you've never been fucked before. I'm going to pound your pussy, I'm going to breed you, I'm going to make it so no other cock will do."

I trembled, slightly nodding in his direction.

"You'd like that, wouldn't you?"

More nodding.

"No. I want something louder than that. Tell me."

"Yes."

"Not yes. Tell me you want me to fuck you."

"Please fuck me," I said, not hesitating.

"Tell me to fuck you with my big black cock. Tell me to fill you up completely. Tell me to change your life."

I swallowed. "Fuck me. Please. With your big black cock. Give me all of it. Everything. Show me what I've been missing."

A low, deep laugh escaped him. "Good girl. Obedient, but willing to fight for her man. Hell of a cook on top of it. Then throw in she's the most pretty ass white girl I've ever seen? Goddamn, Mitch, you're one spoiled motherfucker to have her."

Mitch was barely looking at him. His eyes were glued on me. Seeing me about to get fucked by this behemoth of a man.

Hands on my hips, Devon brought the tip of his cock to my entrance. Its girth poked at my folds, but I knew I was ready. Despite already coming twice, feeling him so near? It was more than enough to get any girl back in the mood.

It didn't disappoint me when he finally thrust in. It was like I was being torn apart from the inside, but somehow in a good way. He didn't let me adjust to him for long. No. This wasn't about romance. This was about lust.

He was going to fuck me, and fuck me hard. Nothing that could possibly be mistaken for making love.

Every thrust was strong, powerful, and sent me higher and higher toward absolute bliss. I was already tender and sensitive from his tongue, and now he was taking me like this? My poor aching body wouldn't be able to take this much.

It wanted to, so it would anyway.

Harder and faster he took me, my breasts bouncing as he pounded at me longer, harder. stronger. This man had seemingly infinite stamina, ready to fuck me like he was some sort of machine.

Or so I thought. Even in the throes of my passion, I caught sight of Devon. He was, after all, only a man.

This pretty ass white girl? I was a hell of a lot smaller than him, so I figured I was hell of a lot tighter than he was used to as well. I could see that I was having quite the effect as he took me.

He thrust into me deeper. Harder. He yearned for more, and really? I did too. The rising tide inside me was a chaotic mess, whipping around within.

Devon leaned in and whispered into my ear. "This ain't enough for me," he said. "I gotta take you harder."

He withdrew from me and, grabbing my sides, carried me over to his nearby bed. He then planted me face first on it. I tried to whip back and ask what the big idea was, but he would answer that without me ever saying a word.

That massive cock of his thrust into me from behind. Not

in my ass, no. That wouldn't do for Devon. Not tonight anyway. He needed to claim me, and the only way to do that was to fuck me in the more traditional sense.

Deep into me, filling me. Pushing my limits. The power within me was growing, the ecstasy filling me, all too ready to explode out of control.

I started to fuck him back as our rhythm was established. Grinding my ass against his cock, urging him to take me so completely. The orgasm was building in me so quickly, so intensely, and I was desperately trying to ride it out a little longer. Not to come on this man's cock so damn easily.

Even when I was immersed in the throes of my passion, I looked toward Mitch. He had dropped his pants, his hard cock in his hand. He was stroking himself as he watched me get fucked by another man. Fucking me unprotected, and with no desire to pull out.

He was trembling in place, and I could already see his cock slick with pre-cum. Part of me wanted to call out to help take care of him.

Devon wouldn't stand for that though. Every thrust pushed me higher, every thrust went deeper, every thrust pushed me further and further along to being a gibbering mess of orgasmic flesh.

Another thrust. Another buck back into him. Another stroke. Another buck. It went back and forth, me nibbling on my lip, waiting for the end to finally come, at any moment... any...

Goddamn.

My entire body was shaking, my bones were shaking, my everything was shaking. Everything was just so damn over-whelmed with bliss right at that moment. I screamed, or something like it. My throat was hoarse, my vision was blurry, and my everything was on sweet ecstatic fire.

Yet even among the chaos of the moment, I felt him

plunge his gigantic self in. All the way in. It quivered deep within me. It erupted with warmth. Endless amounts of warmth. Jet after jet of cum being shot inside me, being injected into me.

My unprotected fertile body.

His hands remained firmly gripped on me from behind, and he was in no rush to pull out. He was fully committed to knocking me up.

This wasn't how I envisioned my family starting. Yet... the idea of being seen with a black child, a visible marker of my sinful escapades? There was something oddly enthralling about the concept.

Breathing heavily, I looked over to my husband. His cock was trembling too. It was a familiar sight for me. He had just blown his wad, and it seems he had blown his wad on Devon's carpet.

Devon, though, was hardly bothered by the mess of his floor. Soon, he withdrew from me. He slapped my ass, and left me a wonderful wreck on the side of the bed. "Damn girl... you're really something. You're gonna make me jealous of Mitch at this rate, and I ain't a man who gets jealous easily."

There was a subtle smile on my face, but I continued to lie there, left to overhear the men's words.

"As for you, Mitch, or should I say, Executive Vice President Miller..."

"Wait, what? You mean it? After the whole drunkenness and snapping?"

"Man, I appreciate someone who can bring me something like no one else can. And a fine piece of ass like that? That's not something anyone can offer."

I couldn't actually see it, but I knew Mitch's response. He was looking on, staring in absolute shock to what just happened.

"Of course, I may request a private corporate meeting in this room again. I may do it quite soon. I shouldn't have to explain myself further, no?"

"Yes, sir."

I was going to get this again. And again. My smile was wide as hell, even as my body ached with the aftershocks of orgasm.

"Don't worry about the mess you made either. I can get a cleaner. As a bonus for your promotion even, I'll let you have this room tonight. Mostly because your girl? She looks like she's about to pass out there anyway."

"Um, okay, yes sir," Mitch kept saying.

"Take good care of her, Mitch. I may want to fuck her, but it's on you to love her."

Soon after, the door to the room closed behind him. A familiar pair of hands lifted me onto the bed, and held me close, even as I was dripping with another man's juices.

Time passed, and I wondered what he was going to say to me. What I should say to him. The thing about being married sometimes though, is that you can communicate a hell of a lot with only a few words.

"I fucking love you, Jessie."

THE END

Get Access to over 20 more FREE Erotica Downloads at Shameless Book Deals

Shameless Book Deals is a website that shamelessly brings you the very best erotica at the best prices from the best authors to your inbox every day. Sign up to our newsletter to get access to the daily deals and the Shameless Free Story Archive!

TAMING A BLACK BULL BY KIMMY WELSH

When Emily and Phil cut loose one night and head out for a long-needed drink, Emily is shocked to discover that her husband has some very kinky fetishes indeed. He asks her to woo the big, black bull that's sat at the bar and she does so with ease, flaunting her sexuality. The trio head back to Emily & Phil's apartment and bull Leon shows Phil just how to conquer his wife, dominating her while cuck Phil watches on and cleans up the mess afterwards.

~

"You were crazier than this when I met you," Emily said, leaning across to her husband and giving his arm a playful slap.

"I've still got a secret side," Phil said wryly, eyeing Emily with a lusty gaze.

It had been a long time since the pair of them had spent time together like this. Emily suggested a drink, just like the old days, for the two of them to rekindle a waning love and inject some much-needed excitement back into their relationship.

"Do tell," Emily said.

Phil's smile remained as he stared into his wife's eyes, then his focus shifted and looked beyond her.

"What?" Emily said, turning around.

Phil's eyes were steeled on the bar behind her. He nodded towards it.

"What?!" Emily said again.

"What do you think of that guy there?"

"The black guy?"

Phil nodded.

"I don't know. He looks fine."

Phil scoffed. "Come on. What do you really think? I want to know."

Emily turned again and looked to the patron with a more critical eye.

"Well …" she began, studying him. "He looks … strong—powerful—confident." She looked back to her husband. "And borderline unapproachable."

"Do you like him?"

"I hardly know him!" Emily scoffed.

"Come on," Phil said. "Tell me honestly. Would you fuck him?"

"Philip!"

He smiled and dropped his chin, then he looked back to her sincerely. "I want to know," he said. "I won't be mad."

Emily pursed her lips and sighed. "Sure," she shrugged. "I'd fuck him."

Phil felt the pang of humiliation hit him and it felt strangely good. He tried his hardest not to show it.

"That's all I wanted to know," he said, looking beyond her again as the stranger at the bar took a swig of his drink and said something to the barman.

"What's gotten into you?" Emily said, looking curiously across at her husband.

"Ever think we need to spice things up a little?"

"Us?"

"Yeah."

"Sure," she said, brushing her skirt beneath her thighs and crossing her legs.

"Tonight," Phil said. "Shall we?"

Emily looked over the rim of her glass and smirked as she took a sip. "What do you have in mind?"

Phil swallowed, knowing this was his moment.

"Go and talk to that guy over there," he said.

Emily struggled to swallow her drink. "At the bar? You're obsessed!"

Phil laughed. "Just entertain me," he said. "I want to see if you can still woo a guy."

"*Woo a guy?*" she scoffed. "I've still got it."

"So show me," Phil insisted. "I want you to see if you can get that guy back to our place."

"*Philip,*" she swooned. "Feeling a little bisexual are we?"

Phil laughed. "Not quite," he said. "I just want to see you enjoy yourself with another guy."

Emily pulled her chair in and looked across at Phil, knowing now that he was serious.

"You mean this, don't you?"

"Of course," Phil said. "I wouldn't joke about something like that."

"You want me ... with *him?*"

Phil nodded simply.

"Now?"

He nodded again.

"You're sure about this?"

"I wouldn't have said it if I wasn't sure. You go over there and prove to me that you've got what it takes. Don't come back until you've got what you want."

Emily reached across the table and held her husband's hand. "Watch me," she smirked. "I'm a damned lioness."

She grinned excitedly as she pushed out her chair and spun around for the bar, clicking her heels across the hard floor as she made her way to her target.

Phil picked up his drink and sat back, taking a sip and enjoying the show as his wife gave him a taste of what she was made of.

He watched her put her drink down beside the stranger and sit on the barstool. In an instant the man's attention was swayed from the television toward Emily, focusing on the mysterious brunette beauty that announced herself from nowhere beside him.

Phil heard her introduced herself. She affected a cutesy, friendly voice and the stranger visibly relaxed and opened himself up to her charms.

"I'm Leon," he said, and he extended a hand.

Phil watched as his wife took it demurely, as though she were royalty. Leon shook it gently, keeping eye-contact on his new prize. He moved his knees out from under the bar to face Emily. It was obvious he liked her immediately.

Phil sat back and watched as the two became friendlier over the next half-hour. As they spoke they leaned further in towards each other until Leon's hand was resting on Emily's thigh and it was clear that they'd broken through the status of strangers to one of curious familiarity.

Occasionally she would glance towards Phil who would nod and encourage her onwards. He was relishing the chance at being a secret voyeur to his wife's infidelity and she now seemed just as keen. She and Leon had really bonded in the brief time that they'd shared together.

Finally Emily said something that caused Leon to look back over his shoulder towards Phil. Phil stared then raised a hand to give a short wave.

Leon looked back to Emily with an expression of shocked betrayal. Emily spoke quickly as Phil kept his place away from the bar. He watched her plead with Leon, leaning in and touching his strong thighs. She stroked her hands up his legs and looked into his eyes as she vied to placate him. Leon looked back to Phil again and then at Emily, speaking in what looked like calm tones.

Phil sank his drink and stood up, approaching the bar finally and entering the conversation.

"This true?" Leon said, pointing to Emily who looked at Phil, awaiting his confirmation.

"It's true," he said.

"You want me to fuck your wife?" Leon asked bluntly.

The barman's ears pricked. Phil nodded.

"Where?" Leon said simply.

Phil leaned forward and spoke quietly, keen to keep the arrangement between the three of them.

"Back at our apartment," he said. "It's a ten-minute walk."

"This ain't no weird shit?" Leon said, as if the scenario wasn't already strange.

"No," Phil said.

Emily stretched her slender fingers up Leon's leg again. "I *really* want to fuck you," she said. "And my husband here *really* wants to watch."

Leon looked to Phil, realizing the nature of the situation now. "I heard about this kind of thing," he said.

"Cuckolding," Emily said.

The realization hit home to Phil. Before now he'd distanced himself from the word, but there was no other way of putting it.

"So I fuck your wife while you watch?" Leon said, getting things straight.

Phil looked beyond him to the barman who polished a glass behind the bar as he tried to make it look like he wasn't paying attention.

"That's correct," Phil said, keen to avoid such vulgar terminology in public.

Leon drained the last of his drink. "Let's go," he said, and he threw a twenty on the bar.

Emily stood up too and the three of them left together, pushing out into the warm night and preparing to do something sinful.

Phil hung back, giving Emily and Leon more time to familiarize themselves.

"Just pretend he isn't here," Phil heard Emily say.

His stomach twisted with humiliation and he swallowed hard, latching on to the sensation and embracing the feelings of inadequate worthlessness. He just knew Leon could offer his wife things that he couldn't.

Leon and Emily entered the elevator of their apartment building as Phil was coming through the front door of the lobby. Leon pressed the 'close door' button and stared through the closing gap as it shut Phil out.

Phil entered the stairwell and made the slog up the eight flights, approaching the door of his apartment and wondering what lay beyond it.

He put his key in the lock and pushed the door open, hearing the giggling of his wife from the living room beyond.

Phil entered awkwardly, looking to the sofa where Emily and Leon were getting increasingly intimate. She had her legs resting over his and his arm was around her shoulders. The pair of them looked to Phil as he walked quietly towards a chair by the window and took his seat.

"You just gonna watch?" Leon asked.

"He is," Emily answered, putting her hands on Leon's strong chest. "Don't worry. It's what he wants."

She leaned in and kissed Leon's cheek, close to his lips. He turned gradually and she gave him another peck, then his mouth opened over hers and soon the pair was in a hot embrace.

Phil shifted his weight in the chair, forcing himself to watch as his wife tasted the flesh of another man. He knew this was the tip of the iceberg. More discomfort was to come, and Phil felt his heart skip to life in his chest as he imagined the ensuing depravity.

In the quiet of the room all that could be heard was the smacking of their lips and Leon's heavy breathing. Phil watched carefully as Leon's hand settled on his wife's big breast, taking a grope beneath her blouse.

"I want you," she purred, looking down on Leon as though Phil wasn't there.

"Come and get me," Leon said confidently, taking Emily's hand and putting it right on his crotch.

His confidence was unrivaled and it served only to make Phil feel more inferior. He felt himself shrink in size as he watched Leon grow, both physically and in presence.

Emily smoothed along the thick cylinder of flesh that was stretched down the thigh of Leon's pants, kissing his mouth as she rubbed him to life.

"That feels fucking big," she said, taking her lips off of Leon and looking down at the bull's big, thick outline that sat in his pants.

Leon relaxed into their couch, pushing his shoulders back as Emily worked him stiff, teasing herself before the big reveal that all three of them looked forward to.

She took a glance to Phil who sat in the chair with a thousand-yard stare, looking straight at the action with a glazed expression. He swallowed nervously and felt the flutter in his stomach as his wife moved her hand to Leon's belt.

Emily kept her eyes on Phil as she slid the leather through the buckle, opening the belt wide and then popping the button at the waist of Leon's jeans and sliding down his zipper.

"That's it, girl" Leon said, looking down. "Get your fucking mouth around that."

Emily slid forward off the sofa and pulled at the waist of Leon's jeans. For whatever reason he wasn't wearing any underwear and it came as a shock to Emily as his giant, black cock sprang up out of his pants like an ebony monolith.

"God-damn," Emily swooned, looking briefly back at Phil to see if he was witnessing Leon's prowess.

"Put it in your mouth," Leon said, taking it in his fist and pointing it out towards Emily's face. "Don't look at him. Look at me."

She brushed her brunette hair behind her shoulders and moved to the other side of Leon, keen to give Phil a clear view of her going to work on the burly black pole.

Leon looked down at his prize, uncaring of Phil who sat meekly in the corner, watching all of the action unfold. He was helpless to stop it, and it felt good.

Emily spat at the tip of Leon's cock and Phil recoiled in shock. She was like an animal as she tackled it, rubbing her saliva along it before ravenously slipping her lips over the tip and driving as much of it into her hungry mouth as she could.

Leon held her chin steady and groaned, throwing his head back to growl to the ceiling before looking back down on Emily who stared deep into his eyes with a mouthful of cock.

Phil swallowed in the corner and rolled his lip through his teeth, forcing himself to watch his wife give Leon the kind of blowjob that Phil could only dream of. He'd never known her be so slutty.

"I want this big, black cock," Emily groaned now, beating it in her fist and snarling at it like it was her prey. "It's mine. It's my dick."

She pumped it against her face and Phil watched her hand slide over it. The contrast of Emily's pure white skin against the dark brown of Leon's was striking.

"I want this in my fucking pussy," Emily cried, then she bit down its length and started to suck on Leon's weighty balls. Leon looked twice the size of Phil in every aspect.

Leon stared across at Phil. Phil's gaze faltered and he looked away, then Leon moved Emily's hair aside and looked down on her pretty face as she slurped one of his balls from her mouth and gasped up at him.

"Sit on the couch," Leon said, patting the seat beside him.

Emily stood up fast, keen to please the bull. She spun and sat heavy in the seat, her legs flying upwards and her dress riding up her thighs.

Leon stood up and got out of his pants and boots, lifting his t-shirt up above his head until he was completely naked. Each muscle was chiseled as though Michelangelo himself had sculpted it from ebony. Emily stared up at him from the couch and drooled. Phil could only dream of getting that look from her.

"I'm gonna give you everything he can't," Leon said, dropping to his knees and putting his hands under Emily's legs.

He moved her effortlessly to the edge of the couch then he pushed her skirt up along her smooth legs until he could see the mound of flesh that sat beneath the crotch of her cutesy red panties.

Leon licked over the fabric. His pink tongue flayed upwards and Emily groaned in response, feeling the wetness of her pussy flood to the fore and bleed into her panties.

She'd need every ounce of her juices to lubricate the passing of Leon's meaty girth.

Emily stared down into the chocolate eyes of Leon as his lids closed over them and he took another lick over her panties, pushing the fabric into her crease until Phil could easily see the contours of her flesh beneath.

"Give me that tight pussy," Leon said, his voice commanding.

He slid a finger under the lining of Emily's panties and moved the crotch aside, revealing the soaked petals of Emily's groove and the kempt fur that sat atop it.

"That's what I fucking want," Leon said, wasting no time in washing his tongue along it. He flicked up off her clit and spat against her flesh.

Emily cooed delightedly and looked down as Leon docked himself over her sex, feeding his tongue into her, out of sight and tasting the juices that he'd effortlessly coaxed from her.

She slapped her hands down onto the couch-seat and screamed, gasping down again at Leon who moved her roughly into place as though she weighed nothing and tongued her flesh more vigorously.

Phil watched on from the corner of the room, seeing Leon tackle his wife's pussy with a command that he could only dream of. In no time at all Emily was shaking with ecstasy.

"You're gonna make me come," she groaned.

Emily gripped the top of her blouse and pulled it down hard as she stretched her muscles and moaned. The fabric ripped downward and her tits bunched up out of the top.

Leon pulled his face off her to look, unable to let the moment pass without ceremony. He moved his face to her tits and started to suck on her nipples while his fingers continued below.

He teased into her folds and found her stiff clit peering out from beneath the fleshy hood of skin. With consummate ease he flurried his finger over the excited pearl until Emily started to bring the roof down with her cries of passion.

Her nipple turned stiff in Leon's mouth and she looked to his hard cock as she felt the climax grip her tight.

Her body shivered and she pulled at Leon's length. It was rock-hard but she could only finger at the tip of him for now. Leon was holding himself back until Emily exploded, and that looked no more imminent than now.

"I'm fucking coming!" Emily cried, and Phil's eyes widened in the corner as he watched his wife's climax. This would only be the second time he'd ever seen it.

Leon's cock shook on his hips as he finger-blasted Emily towards the finale. He curled inside her like a bowling ball and worked his entire arm, pressing on her spongy g-spot until a clear liquid started to sprinkle up wildly from her pussy.

"Fuuuuuuuuuck!" Emily cried, staring down in wide-eyed wonderment as her cum squirted up and scattered down on the couch and carpet.

Her body was covered in it and so was Leon's wrist. He continued without mercy, as though he'd witnessed this a thousand times. Phil could only stare. He never even knew it was possible and yet here was his wife, squirting like a geyser.

"Damn," Phil said quietly, rapt on the scene before him.

"Oh, fuck! Oh, fuck! Oh, fuck!" Emily gasped.

She squeezed at Leon's wrist and doubled over on the couch. Leon refused to yield, keeping his working fingers inside Emily's pussy as the floodgates opened wider.

Finally he pulled out quickly, leaving her pussy gasping as it fired out one last torrent. Emily sank back into the couch and rubbed her back against it, mewling like a pussycat and rubbing her soaked lips.

Before Emily had regained her composure Leon had mounted the couch. He took a grip of his black rod and aimed it towards Emily's face.

She didn't even see it coming, but before she knew it Leon was back inside her mouth and pumping wildly into her.

Emily rubbed at her pussy and moaned whilst Leon fucked her mouth. She embraced the sluttiness and Phil stared on, watching his wife take control of her inner whore. She was like a woman possessed, as though black cock were a drug and she was a fresh addict, chomping at the bit for her next fix.

Leon pumped from the hips. His curved, toned ass pushed in and out, looking as though it was carved from mahogany. Phil could only dream of looking like that.

Emily's hand came beneath and she held at the muscled curves of his glutes, rubbing against Leon's black flesh as though she worshipped him. Maybe she did.

He pulled out of her mouth and she gasped upwards, her face strewn with spit. Emily's hand moved to her pussy and she fingered along the crease, gripping Leon's cock and taking charge as she forced it back between her lips.

Leon took himself back out of her, his big, black cock swinging and glistening in the light. It was coated in a film of Emily's saliva—saliva that was soon to go back inside her as Leon stepped off the couch and put himself between her legs.

"Ready?" he asked, working his cock.

"Yes, Leon," she groaned.

"No you're not," he smirked.

Leon leaned over and ripped her blouse open wider. Emily shrieked, indulging in the fantasy. Leon gripped her panties and tore them off her too, pushing her dress up her body until she looked like a disheveled whore.

Emily held her pussy lips open, bunching her tits together between her shoulders as she stared up at Leon, panting lustfully.

"Fuck me!" she ordered.

Phil leaned forwards, keen to see the moment of contact. With Leon's legs in the way he couldn't quite get a vantage point. Eager not to miss out Phil fell to the floor and crawled the distance until he could see through Leon's tree-trunk legs.

"Get a good look, honey," Emily said.

Leon's big balls swung at the hilt of his cock as he moved forwards. The bulbous tip pressed against the pink flesh of Emily's pussy and she groaned out immediately.

"Yes!"

Leon plunged deep, unceasing in his advances. Emily's flesh spread over Leon's tip, stretching wide and almost at breaking point.

"Fuck!" she grunted, breathing heavily as she felt the burst of pain inside her. It was real now.

Her flesh opened over him and the crown of his dick popped through the muscle. Emily breathed long and deep when it did so and Leon stayed there for the moment, letting her regain her composure and relax around him.

"And the rest," she urged now.

Leon pressed onwards and Emily's eyes closed tight. She felt like a virgin all over again as that impossible blackness burst her open. Phil's cock never stood a chance in comparison.

Phil could feel himself becoming stiff in his pants, but he knew he didn't deserve to pay it any attention. He stared forward from his position on the floor, watching on his hands and knees as Leon gave his wife the ultimate gift.

The thick, slathered shaft eased onwards, dispelling the thick, creamy juices from Emily's pussy that Leon had given her so effortlessly.

It looked so milky and white in contrast to the dark flesh that it covered. Phil bit his lip and watched as Leon plunged all the way to the hilt, resting his balls on Emily's ass below as he docked home.

"There's a good bitch," Leon said.

He eased himself out slowly and Phil marveled at the marble effect that Emily's juices left on Leon's giant cock. He plunged in again and Emily grunted deep.

"That feels so fucking big," she said woozily.

Leon started to thrust in with purpose, easing back out slowly before slamming himself home all over again. Each time he pressed deep Emily's stomach bulged and she shot a gasping cry from her lungs.

Phil stared on from the floor hopelessly. He could feel the pangs of humiliated defeat inside himself, but he could also feel the hard erection in his pants. He didn't deserve to touch it.

"Give it me, Leon," Emily cried, and Phil winced at the sound of his wife calling another man's name so passionately. "Give me your fucking cum!"

"You want that, huh?" Leon asked.

"I don't want it anywhere else," she cried. "Cum in my fucking pussy."

With his orders clearly defined Leon set to task. He worked faster through Emily's crease, gripping her legs and bucking wildly now so that his heavy ball-sack slammed against her each time he hit home.

Phil listened to the clapping flesh grow louder and occur faster. He watched the powerful muscled thighs hold the weight of Leon's body as his hips flung backwards and forwards.

Leon's cock was awash with the cream of Emily's pussy and the pain had largely subsided for her now.

"Give me that fucking cum!" she moaned, tossing her head left and right on the cushion below.

Leon gripped a hand on her tits and squeezed, staring down at the union of flesh. His black cock pumped through the pink petals and Emily's tight core massaged Leon's thick pole until he had no choice but to give in to the sensation.

"You're gonna make me cum," he grunted.

"That's what I fucking want," Emily gasped, forgetting her sensibilities. "Shoot that fucking cum in my tight pussy! Shoot in inside me so my husband can eat it out!"

Phil winced at the words, yet he found the idea strangely alluring. It would be the ultimate humiliation.

"That's what you want?" Leon asked, not breaking his stride.

"That's what I fucking want," Emily groaned. "I want him to lick the cum from your cock too."

Leon shook his head and huffed a laugh. "You guys are fucking crazy."

He continued regardless, pulling Emily down onto his cock and fucking her so fiercely that her tits bounced up every stroke.

Phil crawled forwards, heeding the orders of his wife and getting in position for the grand finish.

"I'm fucking close," Leon announced, staring into Emily's blue eyes.

"Shoot it!" she ordered. "Shoot it in my pussy. I want your cum, Leon!"

Phil sat at their feet like a patient pet as Leon made his way to the finale. He flurried into Emily to the sound of a rapturous applause as their flesh collided powerfully.

"Fuck!" Leon cried.

Phil rubbed at Leon's balls now, working out the cum as

it shot up through the powerful muscle of Leon's black cock and fired deep into Emily.

"Yes!" she shouted triumphantly, feeling the heat coat her insides. "Give me that fucking cum."

Phil fondled Leon's balls and the cum continued to pour forwards. Leon took some of the pace of his strokes until he was pushing his seed deep each time it leapt free.

"Every drop!" Emily cried, unaware of her husband's studious work below.

Leon pulled out and shot one final dribble of cum across her pussy, then he stood aside and turned towards Phil.

"If this is what you want," Leon said, holding his cum-drenched cock.

"It is," Emily said, answering for him.

She bit her finger and watched, rubbing Leon's cum into her pussy as Phil squared himself in front of the bull and took a grip of his cock.

Leon stepped forwards and soon his cock was passing through Phil's mouth. Phil closed his eyes and wrapped his tongue around the leathery flesh, cleansing the bitter cum from Leon's pole and swallowing it down submissively.

"That's it," Emily said steadily, rubbing her pussy as she watched her husband do her bidding.

Leon breathed heavily, his big chest rising as he stared down. He watched Phil clean him up, standing with his hands on his hips as though he was a conqueror. He'd certainly had his way with Phil and Emily.

"Good boy," Emily said. "Now come and eat him out of me."

Phil moved away from Leon's cock and Leon continued to watch in amazement as Phil planted his mouth over Emily's pussy.

She groaned and pressed her husband's face onto her

mound, looking wryly at Leon and eyeing his fat cock one last time.

He put one foot on the couch and angled his waist towards her. Emily reached forwards and gripped him in her fist, mouthing over the crown of his cock one last time as her husband ate the cum from her pussy.

Phil tongued into her and felt the pearlescent, velvety cream of bull Leon flood into his mouth. He smudged some of it back against her flesh but swallowed the rest, feeling it slide down his neck. He thought he deserved no less.

When he was done he sat back and watched one last time as his wife sucked on the meaty black cock of his dominant rival.

She popped her lips off Leon and smiled lovingly up at him, then she looked down on Phil. "Good boy," she said.

Phil felt a burst of joy at having pleased his wife.

"Right," Leon said, grabbing his pants. "Y'all crazy. I am out of here."

He laughed and so did Emily. Leon jumped back into his pants and got dressed in front of them whilst Phil rested his head against Emily's bare thigh.

"Y'all crazy," he said again, shaking his head. "But if you wanna be crazy again, you know where I'll be."

He nodded at the pair of them and turned to leave. Emily fingered through Phil's hair as he lay against her, his fantasy fulfilled.

"What do you think?" she asked.

Phil rolled the last residues of cum over his tongue. "I think we'll be seeing Leon again."

Emily couldn't have been happier.

THE END
Get Access to over 20 more FREE Erotica Downloads at Shameless Book Deals

Shameless Book Deals is a website that shamelessly brings you the very best erotica at the best prices from the best authors to your inbox every day. Sign up to our newsletter to get access to the daily deals and the Shameless Free Story Archive!

ALL IN BY PHILLIPA SAINT

Martin won't step up.
Time and again, when life throws an obstacle his way,
something won't let him stand up and take charge. So he
loses respect, loses friends, loses work, and now he's even
losing his sex life.
His wife Kristen wants to help, but doesn't know how.
Until a nightly encounter in a nearby park pushes Martin to
limits he didn't know he had, and she formulates a plan.
But she needs to know he's on board. That he'll let her go
all in.
Because he has no idea, but the answer to his problems will
come when someone else goes all in… with his wife.

~

*M*artin averted his eyes as his wife's tongue
twirled around his glans, trying to bring his
limp flesh to life. It was one of those times he couldn't find
the guts to meet Kirsten's gaze.

She let his flaccid cock droop out of her lips, but kept rubbing him, hoping to bring him to life as she normally did.

"Are you okay, baby?"

He managed to turn his face to her and nod.

Kirsten stopped. She let go of his limp cock and took his hand in hers, kissing his knuckles gently as she sat on the couch beside him.

"Seriously. You know I can tell. What happened?"

"Nothing, I'm just... I'm just tired, honey. We'll try again later, okay?" Martin took his hand away and got up, pulling his pants up as he tried to step away.

He didn't go very far. Kirsten caught his hand before he could take half a step, and gently pulled at it. He acceded and turned to her.

"Martin. Come on. Tell me, please. Maybe I can help."

"You can't," he said with a sigh as he sat back down next to her. He took his hand to his forehead, both as a reaction to an incoming headache and to half conceal his eyes from her. If the eyes were the window to the soul, his were always completely open to his wife, no matter how hard he tried putting curtains up.

She leaned in closer. "Tell me," she whispered almost seductively.

Martin's hand dropped from his face, falling on his leg with a slapping sound. He forced his eyes closed. "Roderick," he said.

Kirsten sighed. "What did he do this time?"

Martin took a deep breath, then another.

"He just walked right into Hankel's office and made a play for the Beamer account."

"Wait, you have that account."

"And he wants it. The Beamers have connections he probably thinks are useful, or can get him some other opportunity, or whatever. Maybe he just wants to fuck with me, I dunno."

Kirsten put her hand between his legs. "That's my job," she said, smiling. He continued.

"But he gets in there, and tells Hankel all about how he'd be perfect for that account, how he'd NEVER let the firm down—"

"Neither have you!"

"—how the clients love him, and how something like the Wright thing would NEVER happen under his watch—"

"That wasn't your fault, and Hankel knows it."

"I know, but it was my account anyway. It's still a stain. I'm sure Roderick will be using that against me as often as he can. Anyway, he just went on and on like that, until Hankel finally shut him up."

"Good! Let that prick go stew in his own bile. That's the end of that."

"Well… He shut him up by promising to think about it for a couple of days."

"What's there to think? You have the account! What's he gonna do, take it from you?"

"He can, yeah."

"Yes, but he won't. Because you're gonna go in there, and you'll remind him exactly who you are, and why you're the right man for this job."

Martin said nothing.

"What?" Kirsten asked.

"Well…" He shrugged, embarrassed.

"No. Don't tell me."

"I was in the office. When this… happened."

"Oh, babe. No. Please."

Martin bent his head and covered his eyes in shame.

"What did you do?" Kirsten sounded like she already

knew the answer. And after sharing a life with Martin for so long, she most likely did.

"I… tried to cut him off. Explain how he was wrong. How I actually solved the Wright problem, not cause it. How I'm the perfect man for this job."

He looked at her, hopeful she wouldn't press him anymore. Instead, she gave him the look he dreaded. The "I can't believe you're like this" look.

"But what did you ACTUALLY say, Martin?"

"Almost nothing." He sighed. "Uh, ah, sorry but, actually. Couldn't get a word in edgewise. He just kept rolling on with his pitch."

"Martin…" Kirsten shook her head.

"Look, I know!" He jumped off of the couch, animated by a need to defend himself. Yet he still couldn't bring himself to look her in the eye. "I should've ranted and raved and jumped up and down, instead of just letting him run all over me. I know, okay? It's just… Something won't let me. Something inside me just… makes me always just sit on the sidelines, and never step up for anything. I don't want to be like this. I don't. I wish I could change, but I can't figure out how."

Kirsten followed him off the couch and held his face between her hands while he hugged himself.

"Look at me, Martin." He resisted. "Look at me. Please."

She had asked. He couldn't say no to her even if he wanted to. So his eyes locked onto hers, and he tried very, very hard not to let any tears out.

"I love you, Martin. More than life itself. I know you, and I know you're not weak. Somehow you convinced yourself that you are, so you act the part. But you're not. You have weaknesses, sure, and I'll admit a lack of assertiveness is a big one. But you are not weak. I know you can be strong. And you need to act like it."

There was kindness in her eyes. Gentleness. A deep,

abiding love. But despite whatever else he saw in them, he could still see the hidden disappointment.

"How?" he asked meekly.

"I don't know. I know I want to help. I will help, any way I can. But I don't have a how. I'm sorry."

Martin nodded and broke away from her.

"I'm just... I'm just going to go out for a walk, okay? Get some fresh air, clear my thoughts."

"Sure. I'll be here when you get back. Always."

He nodded, and she managed to land a peck on his cheek before he went out the door.

Martin stepped onto the street with no thought of where he was going. The only things in his mind were the events of the day, all the things he had lost in his life because for some reason he didn't have the guts to step up and take what was rightfully his. That and the fact that for the first time, he couldn't get it up for his wife. Another disappointment in a growing list, regardless of what she said. She did love him, and he believed that she meant every word. But how much longer before his weaknesses started wearing down their love? How long until his lack of balls took that away from him too?

His feet moved in auto-mode and took him along familiar paths. He went around the block a couple of times before he found himself entering the neighborhood park. Then he stopped.

It was a perfectly safe place during the day. But now it was night. He hadn't heard anything about anyone getting mugged or attacked there, or anything. But it was still an empty place full of trees and bushes, shadows and hiding places. Who knew what he would find in there? He should probably turn around and go back—

'No,' he told himself. This was a tiny thing, a harmless thing. This much, he could do.

So Martin walked into the park.

His eyes darted to every shadow as he stepped slowly across the path. Aside from harmless creatures of the night, the local vegetation, and the wooden benches, he saw nothing or no one.

Soon the path took a turn, and he spotted someone on a bench ahead. 'So what,' he thought, and kept going.

Then he managed to get a better look at the people on the bench. And realized what they were doing.

Their kiss was deep and passionate. They were holding each other tight, clearly not wanting to let go. Yet they did. And then Martin recognized the woman. It was Ashley, his next-door neighbor. He didn't know her all that well, but they were casual enough acquaintances for him to figure she'd be embarrassed if she and her husband were caught in a nightly escapade by their neighbor.

Which was when Martin realized that the man wasn't her husband.

As soon as they broke off the kiss, Ashley got off the bench and pulled down the man's pants. Martin didn't even see his underwear. If he had any, it went down with his pants. The man's cock stood to attention, hard as a steel rod, pointing defiantly to the sky. He was big.

'I should leave,' Martin thought. He wasn't meant to see this. It was none of his business. And how was he going to be able to face her husband the next time they ran into each other?

But instead of leaving, he took a few steps to the side to hide in the nearest shadow and watched as Ashley took the man's rod in her mouth. Her head bobbed up and down, eager to take in the considerably sized cock. The man moved, and for a moment, Martin thought he would grab her head as she blew him. Instead, he stretched his arms along the back of the seat, his head tilted back and his mouth open.

Martin could easily guess the noises they'd make if they weren't trying to keep quiet.

Ashley lifted her head and looked at the man. Despite the distance, Martin saw the wanton lust in her eyes. Her chest heaved as her hand rubbed the man's cock, looking to finish the job her mouth had abandoned. Suddenly, she got back up and stood in front of him, hiking her skirt up to her waist while pulling down her undies and kicking them off to the bushes as soon as they fell to her feet. Her bare ass caught the light of the moon. It was as shapely as Martin had always assumed, in the few moments he'd allowed himself to consider it.

She got on top of the man, straddling him as she lowered herself onto his prick. He held onto her waist as she grabbed the back of the bench, using it to gain leverage as she immediately started riding him hard. After a couple of seconds, she gave up all attempts to kept quiet, and Martin could hear her delighted moans as she rode the huge cock.

One of the man's hands went to Ashley's blouse, undoing it and pulling out her pert breasts, then taking one in his mouth. She moaned louder and with abandon, and her hips accelerated her riding of his cock.

'I shouldn't be here,' Martin thought. 'I can't be watching this.' Yet he couldn't tear himself away.

Suddenly, his eye caught a movement he couldn't quite recognize. Something stirred behind a bush right behind the two lovers. And someone came out of it.

It was Ashley's husband.

A cold chill went down Martin's spine, and he feared what he could be about to witness.

But his neighbor simply stood, right next to the bench. The man fucking Ashley completely ignored her husband. She smiled at him and blew him a kiss.

And then, Martin noticed the husband had his cock out too. And he was stroking it hard.

Martin's jaw dropped. More than ever, he knew he shouldn't be watching this. He was sweating, shaking.

And very, very hard.

The moment seemed frozen in time. Martin was transfixed as Ashley's husband pulled his dick out and started masturbating a few feet away from his wife fucking another man. The one time the man acknowledged the husband's presence was when he briefly glanced at the husband's crotch, followed by a mocking laugh.

The husband sped up his jerking off. And Martin almost pulled out his own stiff prick right there.

Then the husband's head moved. And for one brief moment, totally by accident, his eyes crossed Martin's.

Martin ran off.

'He couldn't have seen me,' he thought. 'I was hiding. I was in the shadows. He just happened to look my way, that's all.'

But it wasn't enough to slow him down. Before he knew it, Martin was back home, slamming the door behind him, his breath ragged from the effort.

Kirsten got off the couch and headed for him.

"Baby, are you okay? What happe—oh."

He didn't have a clue why she stopped talking. Or why she was smiling. Until he noticed she was looking at his crotch. His hard-on was still very visible.

"You have to tell me what the hell happened out there to get you like that," she said. "Whatever it is, I approve."

She took his hand and brought him back to the couch.

"You wouldn't believe me if I told you," he said.

"Try me." Sitting beside him, her hand undid his zipper and reached inside for his cock. He almost stopped her, but he felt like he owed her for his limpness earlier. Besides, he could use the relief.

"I don't know if I should."

"Of course you should." He could hear it in her voice. She was getting turned on just from rubbing him. He had to wonder how much more excited she'd get if she knew the whole story. If she had been there to see it. "Oh, you're enjoying this!" she said in response to his increased turgidity.

Maybe he shouldn't tell her. It was enough he wouldn't know how to deal with his neighbors. Kirsten didn't need to be awkward around them too. But in truth, Kirsten was never awkward. Ever. And something inside him demanded to know how she'd react to the whole thing.

So he told her. Step by step, every single detail.

Before he knew it, Kirsten wasn't just rubbing him off, she was also feeling herself up. Touching and squeezing one tit at a time as he told her the story, running her hand all over her body, then finally going inside her panties and rubbing herself. Martin almost wanted to give her a hand, too, but he was too turned on just by watching her.

All the while, she never interrupted him. She prodded him along, with multiple "and then" type questions whenever he had to stop for the feeling of her jerking him off. By the time he finished the tale, they were both moaning.

"Did they come?" she asked. "Did you see any of them come?"

"Maybe… Maybe her. I don't know, I can't…"

"Did the man come? Did the husband?"

"I didn't see it."

"Did you want to?"

"Yes."

"Did you like watching all of that, baby?"

"I did."

"Why?"

"It… It was hot. It was so hot…"

Her hand sped up, finally taking his cock out of his pants.

"Why was it hot?"

"Because… I don't know."

"Was it hot because it was in public? And people you know?"

"Yes… Yes…"

"Was it hotter because it wasn't her husband fucking her? Because it was forbidden?"

"I don't know…"

"Yes, you do, baby. Ohhhh. Oh, God. Tell me. Did you like it that she was fucking a stranger?"

"Yes. God, yes."

"Did you like it that her husband was watching them, same as you?"

"God—fuck!"

He couldn't hold it anymore. Spurts of cum jetted out of his cock, dripping all over his pants and Kirsten's hand. She kept pumping him, squeezing him of all his juice. He looked over to his wife, his wonderful, sexy wife, eager to see her make herself come…

And then she stopped. Stopped rubbing him, stopped rubbing herself, stopped everything. She let go of his cock, letting it fall onto his zipper already at half-mast. Then she licked her hand clean of his cum, and that made him stir up again.

"You didn't…?" he asked.

She shook her head, smiling as she licked.

He tried reaching for her, but she held him off before he could reach her. "Honey, I can help you get there," he said.

"You don't need to, baby. I'm the one that has to help you."

"I think you just did."

"No, not with that. With your problem. With the assertiveness thing."

"Oh." Suddenly, every last bit of horniness left Martin, as his thoughts abandoned the erotic dreamland of his evening and went back to the awkward nightmare of the rest of his life.

"It's not going to be easy. But I think I have an idea."

He turned to her. "You do?"

"I do. But… This could get ugly, Martin. I love you so, so much, and I'm scared this could harm you more than help you. I believe it will help, I believe it will do you good. That it'll do us both good. But I'm worried about the consequences."

"Well… what did you have in mind?"

"If I tell you, it won't work."

He leaned back on the couch again and considered it.

Then he held her hand, the same hand he had coated with cum a few minutes earlier, and squeezed it tight.

"I love you. And I trust you, more than anything. I believe that whatever you choose to do, it's meant to help me."

"And if it doesn't?"

"We'll deal with it then. Can't be worse than… God, Kirsten. I just… I can't stand being like this anymore. So if you have something you want to try, I'm all for it."

She smiled. "All in?"

"All in."

"Then we'll do it," she said with one of her beautiful smiles. Then she got off the couch, and guided him by his hand to their bedroom, where they tried for five minutes to make love, and then stopped when Martin couldn't get hard again.

THE NEXT DAY AT WORK, Martin did his best to avoid Roderick, Hankel, and most everybody else. He just closed the door to his office and tried to focus on paperwork. The papers themselves weren't urgent, but he needed to stay away from the comings and goings of the office.

His mind kept drifting, though. He couldn't stop thinking of the previous night, and his fascination with it all. Because beyond the sex itself, beyond the forbidden nature of the voyeurism and the cheating... There was something in it he just couldn't quite trace. But whatever it was, it enraptured him.

He also spent a considerable part of the day wondering about Kirsten's plans. He'd prodded her about them both before sleep and after they woke up, but she said nothing. The only hint was her near-constant mischievous smile. He didn't even know when she would set whatever it was in motion.

So when he headed home, he didn't expect any answers. But he was still thinking about it by the time he got home.

He opened the door, expecting to see Kirsten waiting for him in the living room. They usually left work around the same time, but she worked closer to home, so she was always the one greeting him on arrival.

But this time, she wasn't there. She was definitely at home, though, since her purse was on the coffee table, and her shoes had been dropped by the couch.

"Kirsten?" he asked, loud enough to be heard around the house.

No answer.

He looked for her in the kitchen, in the backyard, in the downstairs bathroom. Nothing. So he walked up the stairs to go look in the bedroom.

Her dress was laying on the stairs, apparently abandoned without a care.

Martin felt a chill go down his spine.

Then he heard moans coming from the bedroom. The

sexual kind. And moans he knew very well, since they belonged to his wife. Was she masturbating? What could've possessed her so suddenly that she left her dress and shoes lying around to get herself off?

He walked up the stairs, and it only took two steps before he heard something else.

A man's voice.

Also coming from the bedroom.

"Yeah, you like that, don't you, girl?" said the voice.

"Yes. Yes, oh, God, yes, give it to me. Give it to me good!"

The reality of what was happening was undeniable. Kirsten was having sex! In their bedroom! On their bed!

Martin was crestfallen. How could she? All the talk about how they loved each other, how they trusted each other, and now this?

He wouldn't stand for this. Not in a million years! He'd run into the bedroom and break it off immediately, giving them both what they deserved—

—which was what? What would he do? What could he, aside from walking in there and telling them to stop?

"OoooooooOOOOOooooOOOOhhhhhh," came Kirsten's undulating moan, accompanied by the quick slapping sound of flesh against flesh.

Martin forced himself to step forward. Whatever he was going to do, he had to do something. He couldn't simply stand by and let his wife get fucked in his own bed by whoever it was!

So he managed to force himself to slowly step up to the bedroom door. It was only half-closed.

He immediately recognized the man inside his wife. It was Isaiah, a colleague of hers. A handsome, extremely fit black man, Isaiah had made Martin feel insecure in his presence from the moment they met at some office party. Particularly since he wasn't shy about flirting with Kirsten. For her part, she pretended not to go along with it, but Martin could tell she enjoyed the attention. Martin and Kirsten had actually discussed it later, and Kirsten had admitted she found him attractive and would be all over him if she wasn't married and in love. But she was both, so she would never let it go beyond what Martin had witnessed.

Except now he was witnessing something far, far beyond that.

He was witnessing Isaiah's huge black cock being pumped hard inside his wife, over and over again.

Kirsten was bent over the dresser, facing the farther end of the room. Isaiah was behind her, holding her hips so hard that it had to hurt, fucking her so hard and fast Martin could see the tight ripples of effort on Isaiah's hip muscles. Then he let go of one of her hips, grabbed her hair and pulled it hard enough for her head to jolt back, bending her neck as far as it would go. Somehow, he was still fucking her just as hard, and she was moaning louder and louder.

Then she opened her eyes and spotted her husband.

Her lips parted with a smile.

"He—Hello, honey. Welcome... Welcome home. Ahhhh, God!"

Welcome home? That was all she had to say? Anger bubbled up inside Martin, burning from head to toe. He wanted to scream at her, insult her, kick her out of the house. He wanted to punch Isaiah in the face, smash in those perfect features of his, teach him not to steal his wife!

But Martin did none of that. He clenched his fists and just stood there. Watching.

Reacting to Kirsten's words, Isaiah turned and noticed Martin for the first time.

"What the fuck—"

"Don't stop!" she screamed. "Forget him, just don't fucking stop!"

He did exactly as he was told, proceeding to ignore Martin's presence.

"Don't... Kirsten, I'm your husband!"

"So? Isaiah's the one... fucking... me... right now, honey. And damn it, he's doing it so... fucking... right...Ooooh..."

"You're not doing so bad yourself, babe. You're a great fuck."

She laughed.

Martin was aghast. It was surreal. All he could do was watch as his wife's body convulsed with pleasure at the touch of another man. She came and howled in front of him, and there he stood, frozen. Just watching.

Kirsten panted as the waves of her orgasm subsided. She tapped Isaiah's hand and he slowed down, then stopped and pulled himself out of her. His cock stood hard and straight. It was easily twice Martin's size, and definitely girthier.

She pushed herself back, just enough to get off the dresser.

"Don't be like that, honey," she told Martin. "You know we talked about this."

"We talked— We discussed a threesome! As a fantasy! We never talked about this!"

She pulled Isaiah towards the chair by the nightstand and patted the seat, winking at him and nodding towards the chair. He smiled and sat down.

Kirsten turned and faced Martin, her back to Isaiah. He made to grab her by the waist, but she shooed his hands away, so he simply waited.

"But this is even better," she told her husband. "Isn't it? Didn't you get off watching Ashley and her men?"

"I did, but that was her, this is you!"

"Damn right it is." She turned around, faced Isaiah, and straddled him on the chair, slowly impaling herself in his huge rod. "Fuck, that's... Oh, God, it's so hard to fit, but it's so good..."

Martin was transfixed. The view of his wife inserting that big cock into herself both repelled and enthralled. Even worse, as her up and down movements increased speed, showing her body was adapting to Isaiah's size, another intense feeling coursed through his trembling body: deep, deep arousal.

Kirsten put her hands on Isaiah's shoulders, moving quicker and quicker. His hips moved to meet hers. She moaned loudly, her head tipped back, so turned on that Martin could see the slickness of her juices leaking down Isaiah's cock and onto the seat. They were going at it so hard, Martin actually feared they'd break the chair.

"Oh, my God," she repeated, again and again. "You're so fucking amazing." Then, to Martin, she said, "Was this how they did it last night? Hm? Is this what turned you on so much? Are you getting turned on right now?"

Martin almost said yes. Then he forced himself to remember who he was talking to and tried to force his anger to overcome his arousal. He opened his lips, but no words came out.

Kirsten looked at him and laughed.

"Oh, Jesus, that look on your face is priceless." She turned to Isaiah again as she stopped and dismounted him. "Let's do something else, this is great but you're hurting me a little."

"Goes with the territory," he said.

She laughed. "I know, but let's go down a different lane for a bit."

Kirsten got onto the bed and locked her arms around her knees, pulling her legs open in the air.

"Kirsten," Martin managed to say between gritted teeth. "You're my wife."

"Sure am, honey. But this is just more of the same for you,

isn't it? You always let someone else come and take what's yours while you stand there and watch."

"I don't—"

"Yes, you do." Isaiah positioned himself between her legs and his throbbing prick immediately found the way into Kirsten. "Oooh, God. That's soooo gooooood," she said. "Tell you what, honey. Don't just stand there and watch."

Was she really going to invite him to join them? Would she dare?

Kirsten pointed at the chair by the nightstand, her words trembling with each pounding Isaiah gave her. "Take a seat, honey. Enjoy the show. I'm sure you'll get a good view of your wife getting fucked! By this huge! Cock! Ooooh, my Lord..."

"That's right, bitch," Isaiah groaned. "I'm your lord now. Hail to the king, baby."

"Oh, I'm hailing. I'm so haili—aaaah, yes!"

Martin felt like he was having an out of body experience. He moved, but it was like he had no control over himself. Some other force was telling his body what to do.

What his body did was sit down on the chair, and watch his wife getting fucked by a stranger's cock, twice the size of his.

His hand involuntarily touched the stain left by Kirsten's juices on the seat. The smell was intoxicating. He looked down at it, and instead found his comparatively small cock making a tent in his pants. He wasn't even surprised.

Watching his wife be taken by another man was turning him on more than anything he could remember.

"Watch and learn, honey." Isaiah had her ankles on his shoulders as he pumped himself faster and faster into her. "This is how wifey likes to get fucked! Not like you do it! Yes! Aaaaaaahhh!"

She looked over at him and must've noticed the bulge in her husband's pants.

"Take it out," she demanded. "Take that tiny dick out. I want to see you jerk off to this."

He did so, far beyond any reasoning or thought. He was in full automatic mode, just reacting. His cock out in full view, Martin started stroking it.

Kirsten somehow managed to scoff while getting fucked.

"See that?" she told Isaiah. "That's the tiny thing I have to rely on."

"Not tonight, babe."

"Damn right." She wrapped her legs around his waist and pulled him deep inside, almost screaming with pleasure. Somehow, his huge cock completely disappeared into her. "God, so this is what a real dick feels like..."

Martin felt his cheeks redden, and he couldn't tell if it was the anger, the excitement, or the embarrassment. He wasn't sure he could tell any of them apart anymore. His cock felt bigger than ever in his hand, and he stroked it as hard as he could.

"Jesus, you're so tight," Isaiah said. "You're squeezing me so damn hard."

"I want you inside me. Every fucking inch of you!"

He smiled and broke her leg lock, pulling out of her. It looked like it surprised Kirsten as much as it did Martin.

Isaiah straddled her chest and held her head up.

"Then swallow it," he said, then shoved his big head into her mouth.

Kirsten was gagging within a second, but did her best to hold on and keep up as he fucked her mouth. To his credit, he did it far more gently than the rest of his fucking would suggest. Martin was almost grateful. Kirsten was gagging, and he wasn't two thirds into her mouth. If he'd gone all in hard, he would have choked her.

Isaiah sighed.

"Nah, you're not used to anything this size. Let's go old school for a bit, then."

He moved to the side of the bed and flipped her around, then jumped on top of her and entered her in the missionary position. Kirsten's hips immediately started bucking, urging him to fuck her, and he enthusiastically obliged.

For some reason he could not fathom, Martin got off the chair and approached the bed, all the while holding his hard-on.

Isaiah's head snapped in his direction.

"No fucking way! Sit back down, man," he shouted as he pointed at the chair. "Sit the fuck down!"

Kirsten let out a trembling giggle.

Martin backed up and sat down.

None of them said much else. The sounds of sex did all the talking, as Martin's wife fucked her workmate while he watched, cowed in his corner chair.

Suddenly, Isaiah sped up.

"Come for me, babe. I'm holding myself back, I want you to come with me."

She moved her hips faster as her hand disappeared between their bodies. Martin had no doubt what she was doing, Kirsten loved getting fucked while touching herself.

Her hips sped up and her breath became more ragged, her moans ululating in the air. Isaiah pumped himself faster and faster.

"That's it, babe. Come for me. I'm gonna come. I'm gonna blow inside you!"

"Blow! Let go! Fuck me and fill me with your fucking big dick cuuuum!"

Kirsten's body convulsed and Isaiah grunted, his face contorting as he let himself go and exploded inside Martin's wife.

Their bodies undulated together, as they rode both their orgasms until they subsided.

But Martin hadn't come yet. So he sped up, his eyes firm on the two bodies in front of him, the notion of another man's cum deep inside his wife's pussy. Within moments, a white, sticky jet spurted out of his cock, mostly falling on his pants.

Kirsten didn't even seem to notice. She was busy kissing Isaiah. It didn't seem like a particularly passionate kiss, and Martin took some solace in that.

The kiss ended, and Isaiah got up from Kirsten in an instant.

"I guess that's it," he said as he took an end of the bedsheet and wiped his cock with it. "See you tomorrow at work?"

"You bet," she answered with a delighted smile. He took his clothes and left, not even glancing Martin's way.

Kirsten let her head fall back onto the bed and sighed, staring contently at the ceiling. For what seemed like forever, neither she nor Martin said anything.

"Do you understand?" she said finally, not moving.

"What?"

"Do you understand why I did this?"

Martin's brain had barely recovered from the events, but he managed to answer.

"No. Kirsten, I never thought—"

She turned on the bed and faced him. "No, shut up. You're not getting it. I just fucked a man twice as big as you on your own bed. I'm still full of his juice. And you just sat there and watched. Hell, you jerked off to it. How does that make you feel?"

Martin felt the shame rise to his cheeks, and he looked away.

Before he could say anything, Kirsten reached over to him and slapped him across the face.

"How does that make you feel?"

"I'm angry, all right?" he shouted and got up, towering over her laying body. "I'm fucking angry that you did this to me."

Kirsten jumped up out of the bed, rushed to him, and pulled him towards the door.

"What the fuck—"

"Get out of this room," she said as she pushed him out.

"That's my room!"

"Not anymore. Your room is the couch. You're angry? Good. Take that anger, nurture it, remember it, and use it to fucking take back what's yours! This isn't your room, and I'm not your wife anymore. Not until you grow some balls!"

For one brief moment, she almost looked about to cry from her own words, but the moment passed, and she threw the door in his face.

Martin punched the door, his teeth grinding hard on each other. He kicked at it with such strength it almost buckled on the first try. His fists balled with fury, he ran downstairs, kicked over the coffee table, and took some delight from the sight of it crashing onto the floor. Then he threw himself onto the couch, trying to will the hours away.

He finally got it. Yes, he would put that anger to good use. He couldn't remember ever feeling that angry. So angry that any embarrassment simply burned away. He felt like he could do anything.

And what Martin would do, first thing in the morning, was march into Roderick's office and put him in his place, then head into Hankel's and show him who is the real asset to the firm. If in the meantime the fury abated, all he had to do was remember his wife being filled with another man's seed.

In the evening, when the time came to return home, he'd go to Kirsten, let the fury abate, and tell her what he'd done.

And then she'd be his wife again, and everything would be fine.

And if sometime in the future he went back to his old ways, if somehow he forgot how to use anger as fuel, well… He was sure Kirsten wouldn't mind some more of Isaiah's big black cock.

THE END

Get Access to over 20 more FREE Erotica Downloads at Shameless Book Deals

Shameless Book Deals is a website that shamelessly brings you the very best erotica at the best prices from the best authors to your inbox every day. Sign up to our newsletter to get access to the daily deals and the Shameless Free Story Archive!

DEEP DARK DESIRE BY SAFFRON SANDS

Although happily married, David requires a little role-play to maintain his arousal during lovemaking with his younger wife, Avah.

Not quite as into her husband's fantasy, Avah hesitantly participates in order to reach satisfaction.

But when her husband finds Rykard, a muscular, athletic man willing to fulfill his erotic fantasy, Avah discovers that becoming a hotwife, may not only fulfill David's desires, but satiate hers too.

~

"Oh...oh..." I moaned as my husband of nearly eight years bumbled his way around my clitoris. It was getting more difficult to pretend I enjoyed our sex. As much as I enjoyed oral sex, a tongue lashing just wasn't the same as a good hard fuck.

David had never been the best of lovers, and now he also struggled to remain erect. Unfortunately, when it came to our lovemaking, I found myself more annoyed than turned on.

Feeling beyond frustrated, I pulled David up from my pussy and kissed him hard on the mouth. The taste of my juices on his lips stirred my desire for him. Groaning, I reached down to stroke his cock and guide it to my aching slit, but all I found was a nearly flaccid penis unable to penetrate a wet piece of toilet paper.

David could see my disappointment. He kissed my right breast then whispered in my ear, "Talk dirty. You know it always helps."

I sighed audibly not even attempting to hide my displeasure. Talk dirty meant talking down to him. A little humiliation always seemed to get David hard, but I loved him and wasn't completely comfortable with his fetish. "You know I don't like that game," I said.

David lightly bit my nipple before replying, "Come on Avah, it always gets me hard." He bit my other nipple roughly. "And then you get to come."

"Alright," I said. I closed my eyes as I forced myself into character. I shook my head and sighed loudly again. "You start."

David sat on the side of the bed. One hand on his cock, the other he used to pinch my nipple. "I'm sorry my penis isn't big enough to satisfy you. You're so hot with your toned body, porcelain skin, and so eager to be fucked. All I ever do is let you down."

"And you're such a disappointment," I said as harshly as I could. "With that tiny inadequate dick, have you ever been able to satisfy a woman?"

David continued apologizing for not being man enough to please me, and I kept pelting him with small dick comments until at last he was rock hard.

Not willing to risk him going soft again, I pushed him to

the mattress and climbed on top of him. "Now fuck me with that tiny excuse of manhood before I pack my bags and leave you for a real man," I said through gritted teeth.

David dropped back and allowed me to wiggle on his rod. Pressing my clit to his pelvic mound, I fucked myself furiously with his dick in a race to climax before he went limp again. "If only you had a real cock, something that I could feel inside of me."

"You deserve a real man," David mumbled. "A real cock, a better cock."

"Any cock would be better," I snarled as I gyrated my hips.

"A thick cock," David said.

"Yes…thick enough to stretch my walls." I felt myself getting wetter as I began to visualize a hot young stud entering my needy pussy. "A long cock that stuffs my pussy so full it aches." I chewed at my bottom lip and gripped the sheets as I felt the heat of orgasm approaching. I rode David harder and faster. "I need a big, thick, black, perfect cock," I cried out as, in my mind's eye, I visualized a large athletic stud pounding my pussy hard and unforgiving.

I felt David twitch then gasp softly. I knew he had come only because it was our routine. Not once had I ever felt him come inside me or felt the hot thickness of his seed fill me up. In fact, David came so little there had been times I had to ask him if he had indeed shot a load.

As we lay in the afterglow of lovemaking, David pulled me close to him. He kissed me on the cheek and brushed my hair from my face. "Have you considered my offer?"

I reached out and took his hand giving him a squeeze. "I have." I rolled my eyes and forced a smile on my face. "It just doesn't seem right though," I said.

"What doesn't seem right?" he asked. "You have my blessing." He chuckled. "Hell, it's my idea, my fantasy."

I inhaled deeply as I rolled over to look him in the eye.

"Why would you want to see me fucked by someone you can't even dream of competing with? I mean...no offense but an athletic man less than half your age with a big, thick cock...there is no way you can ever top that." I scoffed then added, "And what if I'm never able to be satisfied in bed by you again?"

David gently stroked my cheek. "Honey, are you satisfied by me now?" he asked.

I sighed and kissed his lips without saying a word. Sadly, we both knew the answer to that question.

～

"AVAH?" I heard David calling me as he walked in the front door. "Avah?" I heard him calling me once more as he hurried into the kitchen where I was cooking dinner.

"Hey," I said and leaned toward him to get my traditional after work kiss. "You seem excited," I said before returning my focus to the celery I was chopping.

"I have something to tell you," he said as he practically bounced around the kitchen.

"Let me guess," I said then pretended to be thinking. "You won the lottery?" I asked then cut him off before he could speak. "You got a raise?" I said expecting that to be the answer.

"No," David said then pulled me from the chopping board, took the knife from my hand and placed it on the counter. "I found a solution to our little problem." He was grinning ear to ear.

I was confused. "Our problem?"

David looked down toward his crotch and raised his eyebrows. "Yeah...our problem."

"Oh!" I said. "You have decided to try Viagra?" I was suddenly hopeful that our limp dick issues could be resolved.

"No," David said his brows now in a furrow. "Rykard," he said and pulled out his phone. "Just take a look at this." He was grinning again as he pushed his phone to me.

I stared at the phone, my mouth gaping as I gazed upon one of the most beautiful men I had ever laid eyes on; a muscular man, with a perfectly chiseled ebony body. He looked as though he had stepped out of a fitness magazine, and he had a cock that would be the envy of any adult film actor. "He's amazing," I said and handed the phone back to my husband. "But how does he solve our problem?" I asked, but before David could reply it dawned on me where this was headed.

"Now before you say no hear me out." David pulled me to a chair and sat me down. "For years I've longed to see you taken by someone just like Rykard. It's as though he stepped out of my fantasy, and now all I need is for you to agree." David held my hands as he spoke.

"Agree to what?" I felt my mouth go dry knowing what he was proposing.

David smiled weakly then squeezed my hands. "You know exactly what I am asking." He kissed my hands. "Let me contact this man. I'll set up a date so you can meet him. If you like him, and you are comfortable..." David let the thought go for a moment before continuing. "Then I'll arrange the next step."

"The next step?" I wasn't entirely certain how I felt about this.

"Yeah, you know." David was grinning like a kid in a candy shop. "Watching him fuck you."

I looked down to see David's cock was rock hard. I put my hand out and rubbed his erection. He was harder than he had been in ages.

I don't know what came over me. It was some crazy mixture of anger, frustration, and sexual need. I tugged at his pants and yanked his cock out. "Hmmm..." I said as I stroked him. "At least Rykard looks like he is equipped to satisfy me." I ran my thumb over the precome glistening on my husband's knob causing David to tremble. "I bet he can fill my neglected pussy." I felt my teeth gnashing together. "And God knows I could use a good fucking after years of this excuse for a cock." I dropped to my knees and licked him from base to head then flicked my tongue along the top to taste his juices.

David gripped the edge of his chair and let out a guttural sound then came. "I'm sorry," he said as he looked down at me. "Visualizing you with him...it was just too much."

"I'll meet him," I said as I stood up. "But I'm not agreeing to anything more than that right now," I said then returned to the kitchen to finish cooking.

The rest of the evening there were lots of thoughts bouncing around in my head. Images of Rykard flitted in and out of my mind. He was a perfect male specimen and I'd be more than happy to have him interested in fucking me. I'd taken care of myself and my body. Even pushing forty, I could give any twenty-year-old a run for her money, but like any other woman, I was still self-conscious and more than aware of the fact that Rykard could have any woman he pleased.

My thoughts returned to Rykard and I felt myself becoming aroused, but then reality crept in to burst my bubble. There would be consequences to David and I dipping our toes into this world. The consequences could be good for us I told myself, but my thoughts didn't stop there. *Or bad*, my inner voice said...possibly even extremely bad.

I'd seen Rykard's cock in the photo. It was big. His dick may even be thicker and longer than I would be able to handle, I thought for a moment, but then a smile curved my lips. I suddenly felt myself becoming turned on at the aspect of trying to take that much cock inside me.

My smile faded as I considered how difficult it would be to go back to David's dick after Rykard's. Yes, that was my biggest fear...that our sex life would be worse after having a man stretch and pound me to pure bliss. I honestly couldn't be sure I would ever want to go back to our mediocre sex.

I looked over at my husband. I loved David more than anyone I'd ever met. He looked at me as if he knew what I was thinking and mouthed "I love you" before returning his focus to the book he was reading. I closed my eyes and wondered if David would be able to go back to our boring role-playing or would he just want more of the fantasy too?

AFTER A LONG CONVERSATION about David being a member of a rather large Cuckold group, I sat down with him and read the messages he and Rykard had been having.

"His cock is only ten inches?" I said with a raised brow. "I'd have guessed more than that from the photos."

David chuckled and kissed my cheek. "After reading the messages that is your response?"

I scoffed and playfully punched David's arm. "Hey this was your idea. And you know as well as I do that his cock is the main attraction."

He pointed to the laptop screen. "Want to go over the email one more time before I hit send?"

I stared at the screen. My eyes quickly scanning our message as my heart pounded rapidly. This message would seal the deal and let Rykard know where and when to meet us. David had picked a posh hotel for our risqué rendezvous. I was to meet up with Rykard at the bar while David remained nearby watching us. If I felt comfortable enough to move forward, I'd give Rykard the key to our suite, signaling David to go to the room and take his place.

Swallowing hard, I nodded my head. "Send it," I said.

Without hesitation David clicked the mouse. The message had been sent and we were one step closer to crossing into our erotic adventure.

David smiled and brushed hair from my face. "Thank you," he said.

"Don't thank me yet." I giggled nervously. "It's possible that I could still chicken out."

THE NIGHT HAD ARRIVED. I was trembling as I slipped into the new black lace panties and bra set David had purchased for me. He said he wanted me to feel as sensual as I was beautiful. A smile touched my lips as I admired my curvy figure in the mirror. The delicate material did make me feel incredibly sexy.

David sat across the room from me, watching as I put on my silky, thigh-high hose. I turned my ass toward him, bent over, and ran my hands up my legs to make sure they were smooth and straight. As I slipped on my little black dress I coyly said, "I can't wait for Rykard to see the new panties you bought for me." I turned to see David's face. His eyes were wide with excitement like a child waiting to open presents on Christmas morning. I was happy to see that he was happy, but unfortunately I still held reservations. I kept them to myself and stepped into my high-heeled shoes. One more look in the mirror then I turned to my husband. "I think I'm ready. What do you think?"

"I think you look fantastic." David wrapped his arms around me as he kissed my forehead.

The ride over to the hotel was quiet. David hummed to

the radio and I looked out the window. It was dark and the lights were hypnotizing as we made our way to the hotel. By the time we arrived, I was trembling. David put his hand on mine. "You don't have to do anything you don't want to do," he said reassuringly.

I smiled and squeezed his hand. "I'll just need a drink to calm my nerves."

"Well let's get you to the bar." He chuckled before getting out of the car.

~

As soon as we entered the lounge, I saw him. Rykard stuck out among the men at the bar. I was immediately drawn to him by the muscular shape of his body, and by the looks of the women hovering around him, they had been drawn to him too.

David rubbed my shoulders and kissed my neck. "I'll be in the shadows, but I'll have my eyes on you the entire time."

"I love you," I said as David turned to walk away.

"I love you, too," I heard him say then he made his way to a dark corner table.

I straightened out my dress, held my head high and walked straight over to Rykard. "Hello. Rykard?" I said then smiled at the cute little blonde that had made her way to his side.

"Avah." He smiled and motioned for me to sit. "I've been waiting for you."

I melted into my seat. His voice was raspy in a sexy kind of way and his eyes wasted no time scanning my curves. I could see he was mentally undressing me and I trembled.

The blonde scoffed and walked away in a huff. I won't lie. It felt amazing being chosen over a woman much younger than myself.

I put out my hand and Rykard immediately leaned forward to kiss it. "So nice to finally meet you," he said.

"It's nice to meet you too," I replied.

"What would you like to drink?" he asked.

"An Old Fashioned, please," I said.

Rykard grinned. "The lady doesn't mess around." He chuckled then added, "Or do you just need a little liquid courage?" He winked at me then flagged down the bartender.

I squirmed in my seat nervously. "Let's go with liquid courage on the first round."

Halfway through my second drink, I knew that I really liked and even trusted Rykard. I reached into my purse and pulled out the room key. I felt a little silly as I dangled it in the air. Everyone in the lounge probably saw me hand it to my handsome soon-to-be lover, but the dramatic handover was meant for one person only.

I turned to see David rushing out the door. My heart beat fast, my mouth went dry, and I felt a little weak. This was it. I took a big sip of my drink before looking to Rykard.

"I'm ready when you are," he said with his hand on mine.

"Then let's go," I said allowing him to hold my hand as I stepped down from the barstool.

AS RYKARD OPENED THE DOOR, I took a deep breath. This was it. The moment my husband had waited for, and the moment our relationship would change forever.

Inside the room I sensed David's presence. I looked over to the darkened corner and smiled toward the faint outline of him as he sat in the chair.

Behind me I felt Rykard's strong hands on my hips. He pulled me back toward him pressing his erection against me.

That was when most of my apprehension left and I suddenly felt empowered.

I was fulfilling the fantasy of the love of my life while simultaneously being the object of desire to a man that could have had any woman he wanted. I closed my eyes, inhaled deeply, and fell into character just as I had for David so many times. Only this time it wasn't just make believe, this time my perfect lover was here with me, soon David would witness another man penetrating his wife.

Turning toward Rykard, I slowly started to unbutton his shirt.

Rykard smiled and pulled the shirt tails from his waist-band before slipping his shirt over his broad shoulders and tossing it aside.

I caressed his perfectly sculpted abdomen, my fingertips taking a little longer to trace the line along the top of his pants before popping the button.

I wanted to make sure David had the perfect view of Rykard's magnificent cock when I at last released it from the confines of his pants.

Slowly I pulled down the zipper amazed that it was somehow able to hold the massive bulge without breaking.

As I revealed Rykard's thick black member, I heard David gasp. I stared at it amazed at the girth and length. It looked massive in the photos, but in person it was even more impressive.

Gently I kissed the head of his cock then smeared his warm gooey precum along my bottom lip. I turned to look in David's direction and slowly ran my tongue along my lip. "Mmmm…he even tastes manlier than you." I grinned then licked the underside of Rykard's dick from the base to the now throbbing tip. "My poor pussy," I said with a pouty face. "She's so used to such a tiny worthless penis." I clicked my tongue and shook my head. "This cock is going to rip me wide open and fill me completely."

I stood up and began to wiggle out of my dress. Rykard assisted with the zipper then stood back to watch as my dress dropped to the floor. I stepped out of the dress and kicked it aside. Rykard looked me up and down as he got his first look at my curvy body. I could see myself in the mirror and I knew I looked hot. I smiled to myself. I was about to officially be a hotwife.

Standing before him in my sexy new panties and heels, my chest heaved as Rykard approached me. His hands caressed the outline of my hips and waist then slowly went back down to the waistband of my panties.

"You won't need these anymore," he said with a sneer then yanked the delicate material from my flesh.

I let out a squeal. I hadn't expected that but I liked it. It was difficult but I remained standing as he now gazed upon my breasts. Reaching around me he skillfully unhooked my bra.

Without hesitation, I shimmied out of it allowing him to take in every inch of my nakedness. Even with David in the room, I felt vulnerable under his piercing gaze, but that wasn't all that I felt. I also felt more aroused than I'd ever felt before.

I stood in awe as Rykard removed the rest of his clothes, my jaw dropped as he kicked off his boxers fully revealing the entire length of his erect penis.

I was speechless minus a soft gasp as he wrapped a hand around the thick shaft. He stroked himself slowly with one hand as he pressed gently on my shoulders, pushing me back down to my knees.

"Before I stretch out your married pussy..." He paused as he tapped my face with his manhood. "I think I'll sample your mouth first."

He wrapped his hand in my hair and pulled my head back. My lips parted and I felt his massive cock thrust into my mouth.

I let out a not-so-sexy snort as my mouth was filled leaving me to breathe through my nose.

My jaw immediately ached as Rykard's girth stretched my mouth wide. Suddenly, I was very concerned that he may very well rip my pussy open.

Rykard groaned as he pumped in and out of my mouth. "Oh yeah...the only thing better than a married woman's mouth, is her pussy." He held my hair as he continued fucking my mouth.

I felt my legs weakening as I focused on my breathing in order to limit the gagging such a massive dick was bound to cause. Saliva dripped from my chin but that wasn't the only thing dripping. My pussy was soaking wet, wetter than I think I have ever been. I knew I would need the warm pussy juices running down my inner thighs to lube me up for what was going to be one hell of a challenging ride.

From the darkness I heard a soft groaning. I was so caught up in being face fucked that I had all but forgotten my husband was watching us from his corner of the room.

Fingers tightened in my hair as Rykard thrust his cock to the back of my throat. I snorted then gagged, my fingers pressing into his muscular thighs as I gripped him not only for balance, but also to let him know I couldn't take much more of him down my throat.

I closed my eyes, tears running down my cheeks, another rush of juices flooding my already amply moistened pussy, and I couldn't help but think to myself that this was the most turned on I had ever been. I thought of David in his corner, his hand wrapped around his cock, and I imagined this was the most excited he had ever been too.

Rykard pulled from my mouth with a loud pop. I gasped for air as his hands reached down and pulled me to my feet.

With one fluid motion, I was standing before Rykard, twisted so my back was to him, bent over the foot of the bed, ass up in the air.

I felt the sting of his hand slap my ass. "Oh yeah, that is one fine married piece of ass," he said, then I felt his fingers parting my wet folds.

I couldn't help but lift my behind to him, eager to have him penetrate my aching hole. "Mmmm…" I practically purred as he stroked me.

Rykard kicked my feet wider and smacked my ass again. The sound of his hand striking my flesh echoed in the room. "What do you think, David? Does your wife look like she's ready for my cock?" He chuckled.

"Yes," I responded for my husband. "I am so ready for your cock. I've waited so long to be fucked by a real cock." I wriggled my behind as Rykard kneaded my ass cheeks.

I could hear David's breathing change as Rykard pressed the head of his cock to my slit. I looked his way. Even though I could not make out his face in the shadows, I knew he could see mine. I bit my lower lip as Rykard slowly inserted his cock, clawing at the bedspread as he gradually stretched my walls.

"Oh my God." I reached down to play with my clit as Rykard continued making his cock fit inside me. "It's so fucking big, so thick." I gasped at the sensation of having my pussy so full, savoring each and every sweet inch he crammed deep inside of me.

Rykard pulled back, teased my bootyhole with his thumb then rammed his cock inside me.

I let out a soft whimper, both hands full of bedspread, eyes wide at the amazing sensation that coursed over my body.

Rykard pulled out and slammed me again.

"Oh…" I let out a sigh as I clung to the bed. I knew the ride would be a rough one but I really had been clueless about how amazing being pounded by such a gloriously large cock was going to feel.

"Fuck me…fuck my married pussy," I managed to say between gasps of delight.

I felt a hand wrap around the length of my hair. Rykard gave it a yank, using my hair as reins as he rhythmically began to pump in and out of me.

Hot waves of pleasure swept over me. I began to feel the first wave of orgasm building up deep in my abdomen as the thickness of his cock massaged parts of my tunnel that had never been touched.

"Mmmm…" I moaned as Rykard's thumb continued to press on my buttonhole.

"You like that don't you?" He pressed the tip of his thumb inside me. "You are one dirty little hotwife." Rykard groaned then pushed his thumb inside me. "Oh yeah…she likes it when you poke her in the ass." He wriggled his thumb inside me and increased the pace of thrusts.

"Oh…oh…" I cried out as my body tensed up. I was going to come. "Yes..fuck yes….yes…" I whimpered. "He's making me come, David…oh God his cock feels so good…." I was overcome by the aching in my pussy. The jolt of immense pleasure consumed me and I let out a high-pitched squeal as Rykard slammed my pussy even harder.

"Take my big black cock!" he growled as he shot his load.

The sensation was unbelievable. The convulsions of my pussy tightening even more around his thickness, the twitching of his cock as he launched squirt after squirt of hot, thick come inside me.

I felt Rykard slip from my quivering tunnel. He flipped

me over to my back and spread my legs wide before kneeling on the bed by my head.

I felt his cock as he rubbed it along my lips. I kissed it then licked it. I could feel the heat of my pussy on him and taste the salty mixture of my juices blended with his thick seed.

Trembling I reached down to my pussy and parted my lips. "You see that, David? You see how my pussy twitches as his come spills from my satisfied hole?" I licked the head of Rykard's cock as he squeezed out another glob of come. "You could never make my pussy feel this way." I dropped back to the bed exhausted.

Rykard got up from the bed and gathered his clothes. Without a word he entered the bathroom, closed the door and turned on the shower.

I remained still, my legs parted as my husband emerged from his dark corner.

"That was amazing," he said as he approached the side of the bed.

I grinned when I saw he was stroking a rock-hard erection. "You didn't come already?"

"No, I wanted to save this load for you." He grunted as a rope of hot jizz shot rather impressively from his cock.

"For me?" I moved closer and allowed my husband to come on my face. "Mmm..." I moaned as I used my fingertips to spread his come from my cheek to my mouth.

David smiled down at me as I licked his quickly flaccid cock. "I know it isn't as nice as Rykard's, but it's all yours. I love you."

I looked up at my husband, kissed the tip of his dick. "And I love you too."

THE END

Get Access to over 20 more FREE Erotica Downloads at Shameless Book Deals

Shameless Book Deals is a website that shamelessly brings you the very best erotica at the best prices from the best authors to your inbox every day. Sign up to our newsletter to get access to the daily deals and the Shameless Free Story Archive!

THE PROPOSAL BY AMBER GRAY

Roy likes them young.
He can't think of anything better than a 19-year-old girl,
innocent and ready for a man like him to dominate her.
Women need a firm hand.
Stacy's not like anyone Roy has met before. She's sweet and
innocent, but there's something else that he can't put his
finger on.
Before he knows it, Roy is in love. He wants to get married,
but Stacy has a condition that involves a broad-shouldered,
hung Jamaican man.
What happens when Roy sees Stacy ready for another man?

~

I think it's early Sunday morning. I'm not sure.

I let them convince me to snort a few lines of
something, so the world looks really bright. It could just as
easily be Monday night.

I'm watching porn on my big screen.

My fiancé Stacy is beside me on the bed. She's sleeping or

passed out. It's probably more accurate to say that she's been fucked into a coma. Her legs are open, and her pussy is leaking on the sheet.

My mind is all out of whack. It's hard to keep one thought before I'm off to another. There's writing on Stacy's leg. It says that her pussy is for black cock only. I should be mad about that.

I love her, and I hate her. I'm humiliated, but my dick is as hard as it'd ever been.

I want to fuck her more than I ever have before, but I don't want to be where he's been. The problem is that he's been in all three holes. The black bastard was even in her virgin asshole before I was.

All I know is that I want her more than I ever have, so while she sleeps, I watch the video of her being fucked.

～

IT ALL STARTED with my sister Nancy.

"What about women your own age?" Nancy said. As usual, she was being a bitch, always poking her nose into my business.

"Why would I do that?" I asked.

"Because," she said. "You can't just date 20-year-olds. You're almost 40."

"Yeah, you're right," I lied. Anything to shut her the fuck up. There was no way I was going to stop.

The last girl I dated was named Alexis. She had a smoking hot body with slender hips, tight ass, and perfect tits. If I wanted a blowjob, I took her to Outback Steakhouse or gave her a cheap necklace.

We were eating breakfast at a cafe with our parents. Nancy had just announced her engagement, and my parents immediately looked at me as if I was going to magically pull a wife out of my asshole.

Nancy was single. I was single. We could do whatever we wanted. She didn't know a good thing when she saw it. Then again, maybe she did.

Her fiancé looked like he was barely 25.

Still, Nancy wouldn't let up. She insisted that I find some old hag. Alexis said the same shit when she left. Fuck her and fuck Nancy. I was living the fucking dream.

IT TOOK me a couple of weeks to find the next girl. I'd stopped searching for them at the local college. Ten years ago, those girls were ready to "explore their sexuality." They'd do anal without batting an eye and could suck a dick like a platoon of Eastern European whores.

Now, it was different. Educated girls don't suck and fuck anymore. Well, they don't suck and fuck men.

I started paying more attention to waitresses and chicks working at the mall. I never hit on high school girls. Technically, they're legal, but even I had a limit.

One day, I met Stacy.

Stacy really wasn't my type. Yes, she had a face like a fucking model. Her skin was flawless, and her green eyes were like a miracle under thick blond hair.

The only problem was that Stacy was short and plump. I mean, she was 10 pounds from fat, but she was pushing that every day.

But her tits looked huge on her frame.

The best part? She was as innocent as a fucking baby doe.

The first time I fucked her, I thought that I caught a virgin, but I found out that some pimply kid beat me to it.

Stacy worked at a coffee shop across town. It was just

dumb luck that I walked in. I don't spend money on coffee when I have perfectly good instant coffee at home.

I just needed to use the bathroom.

She had such a cute face and fat tits that I had to come back the next day and the day after that.

"I'll be out of town on business," I said. "When I get back, would you like to have coffee with me?"

She scoffed. Who did that bitch think she was? I was about to curse her out when she said, "Not coffee. I work in a coffee shop all day. You can buy me tea."

~

THE FIRST COUPLE of dates were always the most important.

Stacy was going to find out my age--I knew there was nothing I could do about it. She was going to meet Nancy. My sister would try to turn Stacy against me, planting seeds of independence.

Until then, I had to be the perfect gentleman, show her what an older man could do.

Plus, whenever she got on my nerves, I'd just go out of town on business.

Business meant that I was taking a few days off to play video games or whatever.

After she learned where I lived, I would have to actually go somewhere. I'd drive down to Austin, where Tyler, a buddy of mine, lived.

Tyler had the same appreciation for girls that I did, except he didn't have a problem with cruising high schools.

The only threesome I ever had was at Tyler's place with a couple of girls on their graduation night. Tyler took the good looking one, and I was stuck with her two fat friends who smoked up all my weed. I made them kiss while I fucked the slightly thinner one.

I could handle Stacy. I'd been doing this for almost twenty years; she wasn't going to be a problem.

Or so I thought.

~

I HAD A SYSTEM IN PLACE. On the first date, I'd have some heavy petting. Nothing serious, but enough to get Stacy's juices flowing.

If she wanted sex, I'd fuck her. Why wouldn't I?

But I'd end it. I wanted an innocent girl, not a slut.

Stacy was perfect. She kinda went with the flow.

I took her to the boardwalk. We rode a few rides, and I won her a bunny. I had to slip the guy a ten because I wasn't good at throwing a blunt dart at an under-inflated balloon.

We had hot dogs and walked along the river. Stacy went on and on about her dreams. How she wasn't sure if she wanted to open a restaurant or get into fashion design. I pretended that I knew people that I could talk to.

I chatted her up between dates, telling her that I missed her and telling her how lucky we were to find each other.

I can't remember where we went on the second date. I just remember getting my hands on those juicy tits. I fingered her in the back seat of my car. She liked it.

Stacy was so innocent that she didn't know how to masturbate. And, she wasn't religious, so she wasn't looking for a ring. Did I mention that she was too stupid for college? So many odds stacked in my favor.

Plus, I found her in the city. Small towns are full of these bitches, but there's always someone that sees through my bullshit. An ass-kicking isn't worth it for some pussy.

If Stacy wasn't so heavy, she would be perfect. I knew I had a bitch that I could milk for a long, long time.

The third date was when I poured it on. I timed it with her period when I knew she'd be horny.

Nice restaurant. Great food. Wine.

That night, we went back to my place. She was woozy from the wine. I'd paid $30.00 for it, so I guilted her into drinking most of it. Not to mention the cocktails and champagne.

I pulled her panties down and crawled between her legs.

"Roy," she moaned as I slipped into her pussy. She was tight, gripping my penis hard. It kinda hurt, but I had to think of it as an investment.

A COUPLE OF MONTHS PASSED.

I couldn't say that I was falling for Stacy. I was just getting used to having her around.

We'd just had sex on a Saturday afternoon. She had to go back to work.

"You want me to drive you?" I asked.

"That's so sweet," she said. "No, you get your rest."

I fell asleep, but when I awoke, my apartment was spotless. Stacy cleaned the living room, the bathroom, and the kitchen.

Stacy was both a fucktoy and maid! I thought I'd had it made. She couldn't give a blowjob worth shit, but no one was perfect.

"I thought you left," I said when she came through the door.

She gave me a funny look. "I did, and now I'm back."

"Oh," I said. I immediately knew what the problem was. I wasn't in my twenties anymore, and I'd been fucking her every night. I was tired and needed sleep. Usually, I'd see girls once a week and could rest up, but Stacy was becoming insatiable. I started eating pussy to get her to go to sleep. Maybe that's when I should have realized how much I was losing.

There was a knock on the door. Stacy answered it.

Nancy walked in. "You must be Stacy. I'm Nancy," she said. Nancy reached her hand out to shake, but Stacy pulled her in for a hug pressing her fat tits against my sister.

Nancy turned red in embarrassment. I found the whole thing funny.

"I just came for the invitations," Nancy said.

Fuck, I forgot to get them from the printers. They were supposed to be sent out weeks ago.

Before the yelling could start, Stacy jumped in. "It's my fault," Stacy said. "He kept telling me that he had to go, and I distracted him. That's what happens when couples are in love."

Nancy gave me a look, and I shrugged. I could admit to forgetting her stupid invitations or deny that we were "in love," but I couldn't do both.

"Why don't we do it now?" Stacy suggested. "It will give us a chance to spend time together."

I shook my head. This was going to end badly, but there was nothing that I could do about it, so I went back to bed.

THE NEXT NIGHT, we were almost asleep when I heard, "You date a lot of young girls."

Stacy was next to me, snuggled close on a cold night. I was enjoying her cushioning. I guess I was too used to skinny girls who were all knees and elbows.

"What?"

"You don't date women your own age," Stacy said.

I made a sound like I was too drowsy to talk and rolled

over. I pretended to sleep as she rambled on and on. She nudged me a few times, but I ignored her.

I knew the ride was over, and it was time to break up with her.

~

IN THE MORNING, she made pancakes and sausage links for breakfast. She'd insisted on cooking even though I wanted to go out so that I could break up with her in public. I don't know if it was dumb luck or if she knew what I was doing.

"I have a friend who's looking for category specialists. It pays really well. I was going to do it, but none of my categories are open."

"What's that?"

"I'm not sure," she said, then proceeded to tell me everything about the position. Basically, big stores need people who become experts in a product. They might have a person on gas grills. But another dozen doing kerosene, charcoal, electric, wood, and so on.

"I don't know how your business is doing, but if you're not out of town, I guess it can't be doing that well."

My business was mooching off my parents, which was going well, but I hadn't been out of town in weeks.

"You need a degree, but there are ways around that."

"I have a degree," I lied.

I got the job, and that pretty much sealed my fate.

~

"I DON'T WANT YOU GOING," I said. "Why would Nancy even invite you?"

Stacy was getting ready for Nancy's bachelorette party.

She wore a sexy black dress that parted enough to show the freckles across her cleavage.

"She invited me to be polite," Stacy said.

"Then you don't have to go," I countered.

Stacy looked for her missing high-heeled shoe. I'd thrown it behind the refrigerator, not one of my proudest moments.

Okay, I am kinda proud of it.

Stacy didn't answer as she grabbed a pair of green shoes with lower heels.

"But why do you have to dress like that?" I asked.

I did not like the look of pity that she gave me. I was the one who gave that look. I wasn't supposed to be on the receiving end.

"Fine," I said. I sat down on the couch with my arms folded.

Stacy stood by me and tousled my hair. "C'mon, Roy," she said. "It's just a party. We play the dirty diaper game and drink too much cheap wine. Nothing bad."

"I'll drive you," I said. "You don't want to drive drunk."

"I have to go," Stacy said.

In all honesty, I doubted that she'd be back.

I woke up to Stacy pulling at my underwear.

"Stacy?" I was tired and groggy.

The lights were off, but some light came through the blinds from the streetlight. Stacy looked like a crazy woman. Her hair was usually neat, but it stood wild on her head. I've dreamed of a chick jumping on me like that. She was horny and hot and ready for me. I wasn't sure why I wasn't ready for her.

When she finally got my shorts off, she let out a sound of frustration like some kind of jungle cat.

I smelled alcohol on her breath.

"What are you doing?" I asked. I wasn't ready for all this. I was still mad at her for leaving.

She grabbed my limp penis between her fingers.

"Ow," I said as she pinched it.

We stared at each other.

"What? You don't like that?" she asked.

"No," I said.

"Big baby."

I was about to tell her to go fuck herself when she dove headfirst into my penis. With the look on her face, I thought that she'd bite me or something.

I tried to close my legs, but she wasn't going to be stopped.

Where was this when I actually wanted a blowjob?

When her lips touched the head, she sucked me inside her mouth and started bobbing up and down. My arms, my legs, and my whole body went weak. It was like she was draining my life force.

She groaned again, and her wet mouth vibrated as she clamped down on me.

Until that moment, her blowjobs were pathetic. She kissed at my penis, spent too much time stroking, and hardly put it in her mouth at all. Now, she was doing it like a pro.

I was seeing stars.

It wasn't long before I was hard and ready to blow. Still wearing her dress, Stacy climbed on top of me. Her pussy was incredibly wet, and for once, I slipped inside of her with no problem. She pinned me to the bed and rode me like the world was going to end.

"Suck my tits," she said. "Suck them hard."

I did, but she grabbed a handful of my hair. "I said hard."

She slammed down on me again and again. I kept slipping out of her, but she put me back in and kept going.

I don't know if she came, but I know I did.

"We're not done," she said when I tried to roll over.

I don't know what kind of demon had possessed her. The girl that wouldn't touch my penis until after I showered took me into her mouth after I'd been inside her. She made nasty, slurping noises as she fingered herself.

She got on all fours and made me fuck her from behind.

"Deeper, baby," she yelled, but that was as far as I could go.

~

THE NEXT MORNING, Stacy was hungover. She scrambled eggs, made toast, and fried up sausages. She even made coffee, something that she never did.

"How was the party?" I asked.

"Fine," she said.

I waited for more of an answer. When she didn't give one, I asked, "Where did you go?"

"We spent most of the night at Barbara's house. I guess she's Nancy's friend."

"Fat Barbara?" I asked. "She's our cousin."

"It's not nice to call her fat."

I didn't say anything to that. I wasn't going to spend my Saturday morning arguing about whether my fat cousin was fat or not.

"What else did you do?"

"Restaurant and dancing," she said.

"What kind of restaurant?"

"Mexican."

And that was the whole conversation. She was stonewalling me. Giving no details so I couldn't catch her in a lie. I couldn't believe she was doing it. I invented that.

I dropped it and ate my eggs. Stacy had this smile on her

face that told me there was more to the story than I probably would ever know.

~

THAT NIGHT I took Stacy out. When I asked what she wanted to eat, she said, "Jamaican."

That was another red flag that I should have caught. I dated young girls for a long time. They're adults, but they ate like children. I bought more chicken nuggets, pizza, burgers, and pancakes than I care to count. Not one of them ever asked for anything that wasn't American except for tacos.

She chose the place, and we went to eat. The food was okay. I had jerk chicken, rice, and beans. Stacy ordered tacos.

The place was full of black people. Some of them sounded like they were from the islands and others from down the street. We were the only white people in the room.

The owner came out to meet us. He was tall and looked like a linebacker for the Steelers. His skin was dark.

"Stacy, is it?" he asked.

"Yes," she said.

"I hope you and your friends had a good time?" the man asked.

He looked at me and smiled. "This must be your husband. I am Desmond," he said, reaching to shake my hand.

I shook but squeezed his hand as hard as I could. It was like squeezing a brick.

"I thought you said you went for Mexican food?" I asked her.

Stacy blushed. I knew that I caught her in a lie.

"Americans get confused. They think everything south of the border is Mexican. Her friend Barbara also is funny that way."

"You mean fat Barbara?"

Desmond gave me a look.

"What?" I asked. "Can't take a joke?"

"No, cannot," he said, going very cold. "Barbara is a beautiful woman who deserves respect."

I threw up my hands. I'd had enough of the bullshit. Between Stacy going out all night and this asshole telling me what I can and cannot say, I was through.

"She'd fit in here," I said.

I waved my hand around. All the waitresses were fat or big-boned or whatever. They were just like the customers.

I wasn't thin, but I was a man. It was different for me.

Desmond should have understood that and given me a high five. Instead, he shook his head. "You have a good evening."

"That was mean," Stacy hissed.

"Fuck that," I said. "I'll just leave a bigger tip."

I looked around. The restaurant was small, with too many tables for the room. The place smelled like cooked beans and served only beer and wine. How was Desmond going to make any money without hard liquor?

"I'm going to apologize," Stacy said. She got up, and I ordered another beer.

When she came back, I had two empty bottles in front of me. "Did you apologize?" I asked.

I expected her to snap at me. I was picking a fight, but she didn't take the bait.

"Let's go," she said. She was using her sad voice. For a moment, I felt terrible. I mean, I was being the asshole, but fuck that.

Outside, she insisted on driving.

"No," I said. She never drove the Charger, and after how she acted that weekend, she wasn't going to start.

"You're drunk," she said.

"I'm not drunk."

Stacy sighed heavily. "You've been drinking."

I got in the car. It was a bad neighborhood, and I knew that I had her. "Either get in the car now or stay here."

She didn't argue. Stacy walked back into the restaurant.

Fuck that bitch.

~

I WILL NEVER DRIVE after drinking again. I wasn't drunk, but Stacy was right. I had a few drinks.

I took a corner too fast, and now my car doesn't have a headlight. Someone's car is a bit fucked up, but it was a couple of miles from my apartment, so I kept going.

I tried to call Stacy on Sunday. She wouldn't answer the phone. When I texted, I saw that I'd sent some nasty messages the night before.

I called her fat.

A week later, I calmed down and texted that I was sorry, and if she wanted to break up, then I wouldn't fight her.

The funny thing is that during those days, I realized how much I loved her. I mean, I really loved her.

I drove to her job and had the good sense not to go in. I waited in the car until she came out at the end of her shift. I was lucky that she didn't call the cops.

"You want me to take you back?" she asked.

"Please."

Stacy sighed heavily. "I'll think about it, but I'll have a condition," she said.

"Anything."

~

STACY TOOK ME BACK, and I couldn't have been happier.

It was just in time for the wedding, so I bought Stacy an

engagement ring. It just seemed like it was time to settle down, and Stacy was everything I wanted.

I knew a good thing when I saw it.

For someone that was such a bitch all the time, Nancy was beautiful. She got everything that she wanted in that wedding. They'd rented the enormous Catholic church downtown and the reception hall at the fancy hotel across the street. All our relatives came with piles of gifts. It was the first wedding in our family in years, and Nancy took full advantage.

The funniest part was that I didn't realize how much taller than her fiancé Nancy was. She had to lean down for him to kiss her. I choked back laughter. Stacy hit me, but she was holding my hand. It was great.

During the dinner, it was my turn to give a toast, so I stood up. Stacy touched my hand.

"Now's not the time," she said.

I immediately knew she was talking about the ring.

Later, Stacy and I sat on the couch. She wore a skimpy white nightie and white panties. We were watching a sci-fi movie when she said, "Why don't you play some porn?"

∼

"REALLY?"

"Sure, baby," she said.

Another red flag.

Young girls were either totally against porn, or they loved that I loved it. Mostly, they hated it. I thought that I was the luckiest man in the world.

I connected my phone to the big screen and opened a folder of videos.

"Go ahead," she said when I hesitated. "I won't judge."

I played her a few of my favorites as we snuggled on the

couch. We watched as older men seduced young girls. They were all legal age, of course. The videos were amateur stuff. Most were shot in bedrooms and cars. The girls were so stupid sometimes that they were cross-eyed.

Stacy stroked me as we watched. She whispered in my ear, and her hot breath made me crazy.

"You like them young, don't you?" she asked. "Young like me? Ready to do anything for you?"

I nodded, unable to speak.

Stacy was doing everything I hated in a woman. She was taking control, dominating me, but it was driving me crazy.

"You know if you want, I'd fuck a girl for you. Would you like that?"

I smiled. It was a crazy thing that she'd never do.

"I'd do it. I run my fingers up her body until her nipples were standing up, and she was running hot."

I almost came then. Stacy must have felt it because she slowed down her stroking.

"I'd fuck a black man for you," she said.

I should have sat up or protested or stopped her. She licked my neck and bit me hard enough to leave a mark.

"I'd suck his cock like it was the last cock in the world. You'd love to see that black dick between my pretty pink lips."

I shook my head.

Stacy didn't say a word. She simply took my phone and scrolled to a different video. On the screen, a large black man with midnight dark skin fucked a pale white woman. She was thin but had big fake tits that flopped with each thrust. She was on her back with her legs open.

The couple had been making videos for years of the wife with another man. The men were always black with skin from tan to charcoal, but the darker the skin, the hotter the video.

"You want me to fuck a black man," she said. "You want him to cum inside me, watch it leak out of me."

She massaged my balls as she stroked me. Her touch wasn't gentle.

"Tell me you want me to fuck a black man."

I nodded.

"Say it," she said.

At that moment, I realized that I'd lost it. So many girls had gone through my apartment. I treated them like dogs, took their virginity, and made them suck me off when they hated the very idea of swallowing cum. When I was done, I left. I had all the power. I could do whatever I wanted.

The door opened, and Desmond walked in. It was one thing to see him in a restaurant, but something entirely different for him to be in my house. He seemed to take up the whole room.

"You tell him?" Desmond asked.

"I was getting there," my girlfriend said.

"What the fuck is going on? Why is he here?" I wasn't a complete idiot. I knew what was going on, but I couldn't believe it. I tried to get up, maybe reach for my phone, but Stacy literally had me by my balls.

She looked me dead in my eyes and said, "Now's not the time."

"What the fuck does that even mean?" I asked.

She didn't answer.

Desmond sat in a chair and put a small mirror on the coffee table. It only took him seconds to measure lines of white powder. They both snorted some.

Desmond offered me a bit. I shook my head.

He shrugged and stood up. Whatever he was packing snaked down the leg of his pants. It took Stacy a few seconds to pull out his cock.

It was the biggest cock I'd ever seen. Stacy immediately

went down on it, taking more of it down her throat than a human should be able to.

The sight of the jet-black cock disappearing between her pink lips and into her white face was incredibly hot.

Stacy peeled off her panties and opened her legs wide for him.

I watched helplessly as he put the head against her pink slit. She was wet.

"You all got some crazy fucked up shit going on here," Desmond said.

"Don't worry about it," Stacy told him. She grunted when he pushed his log inside her. "Jesus, that's big."

It took forever for him to work into Stacy.

"He's so big," Stacy said. "He's really stretching my pussy."

I stroked my dick and listened and watched. It was the most humiliating thing I'd ever done.

Desmond began to fuck her, saying nasty things like how he was going to take her asshole next and make her swallow his dick in the middle of his restaurant.

Stacy's body seemed to lose control.

Desmond folded her with her knees up to her chest. Her pussy was so wet that it made sloshing noises.

"Now's the time," Stacy said to me, and I didn't understand what she meant. She tried to repeat it, but she was hit with an orgasm that made her suck in a long breath.

"Get the ring," she said.

I couldn't believe it. Stacy wanted me to propose while she was being fucked by another man—and a black man at that.

"That's the price," she said between grunts and groans. "Either you ask me before he comes, or you can forget it."

Fuck that, I thought. There was no way I was asking her to marry me while she was cheating on me.

∼

A FEW MINUTES LATER, I knelt and asked Stacy to be my wife. She said yes just before Desmond thrust deep and let out a choked groan. He came inside my fiancé.

Stacy was happy. She cried and pulled me closer so that she could kiss me and hug my neck.

Desmond decided that he needed his dick sucked. He also wanted to fuck Stacy's ass that night. I picked her up and carried her to our bed.

As I carried her, Stacy put on the ring. "Bring your phone," she said. "I want pictures and video."

I got the phone, and that was the start of our marriage.

THE END

Get Access to over 20 more FREE Erotica Downloads at Shameless Book Deals

Shameless Book Deals is a website that shamelessly brings you the very best erotica at the best prices from the best authors to your inbox every day. **Sign up to our newsletter** to get access to the daily deals and the Shameless Free Story Archive!

ON THE PROWL AGAIN BY ZOE MORRISON

Sherry has finally graduated high school and is ready to move into her first apartment. Unfortunately, her stepfather still has control, and she has to work for him and make sure he's happy if she wants to spread her wings.

This is my last chance, I thought to myself as I entered the doorway to Temptations. It was Saturday night and I was out once again trolling my usual grounds for prospects. I saw a few heads turn my way as I entered the room, ogling me, but they weren't what I was looking for. I had become quite choosy lately.

This had become a regular thing for me. At least once a month for the last year I'd been making the circuit of about three different bars and clubs near my home. I needed to stay close enough to home to make this work.

I was always alone, hunting, looking for just the right guy. I was doing this because of my husband; he had driven me to this. This was my way of repaying him. *He'll get what he deserves!* I thought as a sly smile crept across my lips.

My usual targets were younger men, but not so young that they wouldn't take the bait. Ideally, I looked for a guy between 30's to mid-40's, unattached, looking for a good time for just the one night. The establishments that I trolled were not only near my home but also close to the nearby hotels. Most of the guys I found were traveling on business, bored and looking for some fun. I could give that to them!

My name is Mya. I'm in my late-twenties, average height with long blonde hair. Most guys think I'm much younger because I make an effort to keep myself in very good shape. At the risk of sounding immodest, I will say that I have a great body: 40D breasts, 26-inch waist, and a firm round butt over shapely legs. My body is well-toned, and I like to show it off.

I tried to improve my prospects and play up my natural gifts by wearing very sexy clothes on these little jaunts. Tonight, I was wearing a very short skirt, above the knee, with a particularly high slit that showed off my legs and left little to the imagination. My white blouse strained at the buttons to contain my large breasts, and the fine fabric provided a glimpse of my lacy bra beneath. I completed my outfit by applying bright red lipstick that I hoped conveyed that I was ready and willing for anything.

But now I was worried that I would come up empty tonight; maybe my standards had become too high. When I first started doing this about a year ago, I was simply looking for the handsome ones, in good shape with a nice body. After a few successful pursuits, I realized that what is most important to me is to find a guy that is well hung and hopefully knows how to use it. It was on my fifth time out that I met a youngish black man that seemed to fit the bill.

It was kind of like tonight, I had been everywhere else with no luck and was about to quit when I noticed this handsome black man, Cole. He was younger than I usually get them, around mid-20's, but I had never been with a black guy before, never even considered it, but Cole caught my eye that night and I was intrigued. As I worked on picking him up I could tell he was well hung, a quick brush of my hand over Cole's crotch under the table convinced me of that. At the time, the thought of 'forbidden' interracial sex gave me a thrill. I also imagined that it would send my husband over the edge.

I took Cole back to my quiet, dark house and that's when I discovered he had the biggest cock I had ever experienced. Was this just luck, or was the old myth actually true, I wondered? Cole was skilled at lovemaking and he rode me for hours, filling my pussy with his magnificent black cock. That night was so satisfying to me that the next time out I went looking just for a black man. I had some very good luck that night as well; I found another well-endowed black man that wanted to fuck me.

So, this had become my new modus operandi: hunting for smooth young black guys! I'll admit that the myth hadn't held true every single time. Sometimes I was slightly disappointed by what I found when I got them back to my house, but I was usually able to weed out the duds before I got around to taking them home. A little 'area surveillance' always helped; under the bar table, in the alley behind the club, wherever.

After several successful encounters, I found myself becoming more and more attracted to these well-hung young black men. I found them to be good lovers, and their large cocks filled me up nicely.

~

TONIGHT WAS no different than my other recent attempts, except that I wasn't having much luck. I was now in my third and last establishment of the evening and it wasn't looking promising. I decided to grab a seat at the bar and have a drink and give it another 30 minutes before calling it quits. After about five minutes I perked up as I saw an attractive young black man, early 30's, enter and grab a booth nearby.

He was tall, well-dressed, even a little nerdy in a turtle-neck and houndstooth jacket, but quite handsome and some-what athletic. I decided to make my move and started to get up from my seat when I noticed another black man enter. Houndstooth waved him over. Damn! This probably wasn't good for me; I expected their two wives or girlfriends to come walking in at any moment. I sat back down to wait and watch.

The two men ordered drinks and just sat and talked. Houndstooth's friend was a little shorter, but more solidly built. I guessed he was a high school athlete of some kind some years ago by his build; strong-looking shoulders and arms. Kinda like a swimmer. Mr. Swimmer had a nice face. I liked them both by sight, and on any other night I would have jumped at the chance to pursue either one, but I figured I would be wasting my time trying to barge in as a third wheel and try to pick one of them up for the night.

It was at that moment that the thought of fucking both of them at once first occurred to me; I felt a twinge in my pussy! I immediately realized that it was a crazy idea! I've never tried anything like that before; of course, I hadn't tried fucking black guys until just recently, I also thought.

Oh, what the hell! What have I got to lose? I also pictured being caught by my husband in our bed with two black studs fucking me at once. That might just about kill him! I smiled again at the thought and decided to make my move.

∼

I LEFT my seat and circled the main bar area to approach their booth from the side. As I neared the booth, Mr. Swimmer glanced over at me and then did a small double-take; I get that a lot. I gave him a quick, casual smile, but then I "accidentally" dropped my handbag to the floor. I feigned a look of irritation and then turned my back to their booth and slowly bent from the waist to pick it up.

I could feel Mr. Swimmer's eyes locked on my ass, and I could just hear him whispering to Houndstooth to "catch that piece of ass!" I discreetly looked over my right shoulder to make sure I had their complete attention and then I quickly stood up and turned toward their booth. Mr. Swimmer had been quick enough to look away at the last moment, but I caught Houndstooth, open-mouthed still looking at where my ass had been before his eyes shot up to meet my gaze.

"Like what you see, fella?" I said, acting a little put out by their obvious sexism. Mr. Swimmer snickered at his friend getting caught red-handed.

Houndstooth looked sheepish and looked away for a second before looking back at me and saying, "I'm sorry, Ma'am! I was just startled by your...um, I mean when I saw you...Excuse me, Ma'am, please don't be mad, but it's just that you are very pretty!"

I took a few steps over to the edge of their table and said, "Two things, Sweetie. Please don't call me Ma'am. I hate that! You can call me Mya." I put out my hand to shake his, and he took it in his big strong hand. I smiled and continued, "And I'm not mad. How could I be when two such handsome young guys say I'm pretty. Of course, only you said that, didn't you?" I said to Houndstooth. "Your giggling friend has been very quiet so far."

I turned to my right and Mr. Swimmer quickly took the hint and said, "Oh, I agree, Ma'am...I mean Mya." He gave me another once over with his eyes as he was regaining his composure. I could sense that he was the bolder of the two. "In fact, Mya, I would say you're not just pretty; you are smokin' hot!" He gave me a naughty smile and said, "By the way, my name is David, and my staring friend here is Gary. Can we buy you a drink?"

"I would love that!" I said. "Move over Gary." I slid in next to him in the booth, pressing myself against his body. I leaned forward, and as I spoke I noticed David had a hard time keeping his eyes off my tits. I ordered a drink and began pumping the guys with questions to see if they were possible candidates. I'm sure they just thought I found them very interesting, but I had to find out quickly if these guys were the right choice.

After the first five minutes, I thought, "So far so good." I learned that they were in town together for a sales convention. They were not only coworkers but also had been friends since high school. I thought that would create a tight bond between them. They have experienced a lot of their lives together and this could be another adventure they could share.

Best of all, they weren't tied down. Gary was between girlfriends and David had been divorced for just about a year. I could tell that they found me attractive and I was giving them all the right encouragement, like overtly laughing at their jokes and complimenting their looks.

I also made sure to make plenty of physical contact; inno-cent little touches and caresses on their arms, hands, and shoulders. But there was still one last test and I had to dive deeper into the pool to make it work. After we had been together for about fifteen minutes I asked, "So, would you two fellas be up for a good time tonight, away from all these people?"

David looked at me hungrily and Gary was catching on quick. I continued, "I am feeling a strong urge tonight and I need someone to help me satisfy it. I like you guys a lot, and..." I had slipped off one of my heels below the table and while I spoke I was simultaneously running my foot up David's leg and thigh while my left hand was moving up Gary's thigh. I had reached their growing bulges by the time I finished my sentence with, "and I know you would like me!"

They both jumped, and I smiled, partly because I was enjoying the moment but mostly because I was very happy with what I was feeling. They both passed my test with flying colors. Gary looked a little nervous and started to say, "Wow. I'm not sure... I mean, we..."

I focused my gaze on David and he was staring right back at me. I said, "If you don't want to, I understand. It's just that I have always wanted to fuck two guys at once and this would be my first time. Maybe we should just forget..."

"We'll do it! Won't we, Gary?" David took the bait and blurted this out while looking only at me. Then he composed himself a little and said, "We would love to spend the evening together with you, Mya; just the three of us!"

I smiled and said, "Good! C'mon, I live just a few blocks from here. Let's go to my house and have a nice little private party." I grabbed Gary's hand and pulled him out of the booth. David needed no urging and he followed me out the door.

～

WE TURNED the corner off the busy main street and onto a

smaller side street that soon gave way to apartment build-ings. I was walking between them, holding both their hands and leading them onward. The street grew darker and I started talking about what I was going to do with them. "I can't wait to get you both at home, in my bedroom! I want to feel you both deep inside me!" I let go of their hands and pulled Gary toward me and gave him a deep, open-mouth kiss.

I figured Gary needed the most encouragement, so I reached down and grabbed his cock through his pants and gave it some strokes. I was surprised by how long it felt. Then I felt David's hands on my ass, so I turned around to give him the same treatment, and I was pleased to confirm he was similarly endowed. I stopped the kiss and pulled them onward. "Just a little further!"

We reached my front walk and I took them to the door. Once inside I shut the door and we stood in the darkened entryway. This time I grabbed David first and pushed him against the wall and started to kiss him and fondle his cock through his pants. I then pulled Gary closer, next to David, and proceeded to feel up both of their cocks while trading kisses back and forth between the two men. I could feel them growing bigger and harder in my hands. I just couldn't wait any longer.

I lowered myself to my knees and started to simultane-ously unbuckle their pants with both hands. I whispered up to them as they watched me, "I have a confession! I have never sucked a black cock before!" It was a lie, of course, but I thought they would like to hear it, so I continued to sweet-talk them. "I've always wanted to! My white girlfriends all tell me that they have tried it and loved it. They all wish their husband's cocks were that big!"

By now I had opened their pants and was starting to pull down the top of their underwear. I wasn't lying when I expressed a gasp and said, "Oh my God! My girlfriends were right! You both have huge cocks! I can't wait for you to fuck me!" Only the top half of their cocks were exposed above their partially opened pants, but it was enough for me to see how enormous their cocks were.

I continued to compliment them, "My girlfriends will be jealous when I tell them I got the two biggest black cocks of all!" As I started to move my mouth closer to the head of David's cock I said, "Oh my God, you are so much bigger than my husband's puny little cock!" And with that, I closed my mouth over the head of his cock and started to eagerly suck and stroke him.

It took several seconds for it to sink in. Gary responded quicker than David; it took David a little longer to understand what I had said since I was busy tonguing him fiercely. Gary said, "Whoa! What?" A few seconds later David understood, and he grasped my head and pulled me back off his cock.

I looked up with a quizzical expression on my face. David looked very concerned and was pulling up his pants as he said, "Husband! What husband? You're married?"

I quickly tried to calm him down. "Yes, but don't worry, baby! He's not here. He'll be gone all night!"

They weren't comforted by this. Gary asked, "But if you are married, why bring us here?"

I took a deep breath and sighed. I slowly stood up, looked at them both and said, "Because my husband is a real son-of-a-bitch, that's why! He cheats on me! He treats me horribly and he rarely touches me anymore! Actually, I'm glad about that, because he doesn't know how to make love anyway!"

David said, "But what if he comes home? Mya, I'm sorry, but we don't want to get in a fight here. I think we should leave, Gary!" As he was finishing buttoning his pants back up he added, "And if he's so bad, why don't you just divorce his ass?"

I grabbed his arm and quickly said, "No, no! Please don't leave! He will be gone all night and I don't want to be alone! He leaves me every Saturday night and goes to play poker, or whatever, with his other scumbag friends, but I know that what they're really doing is going to the whorehouses. He's probably fucking some prostitute right now. He never gets home before sunrise and he always stinks of cheap perfume."

I started to tear up as I continued, "I can't just leave him because I'll lose my house! I'm a nurse and my job pays for everything; my husband doesn't work, and he is just a leech. I've already tried speaking with several lawyers and they all agree that even if I can prove he's a louse, I will still lose a lot in the divorce. I've worked too long and too hard to just give up everything now. I'm just biding my time until I can figure out a better way to dump him.

"And until that day, I am getting my revenge against him however I can!" Then my tears came fast and furious, "But I'm also lonely! That's why I do this. I'm getting back at him, but I also get to feel someone, to touch someone. I get to meet nice people, people like you and Gary!" I started to cry harder and I threw myself into Gary's arms.

Gary reached out to hold me, and I pulled him tightly to me. I stopped crying and I looked up into his face and I said, "Thank you!" He smiled, and I reached up and lovingly placed my hands on his face and pulled him to me and gave him a soft kiss that lasted for a long time. Then I turned toward David, but he still looked cautious.

David said, "I don't know, Mya. What if your husband comes home early? I like you, and your husband sounds like he deserves whatever you can do to him, but we aren't looking for a fight."

I grabbed David and held him. "He won't! I promise!

Please don't leave me alone!" I began to kiss David and the longer it went the more I could feel his resolve weaken. I said, "I was so happy to meet you and Gary tonight. I could tell you are both decent guys and I knew we could have some fun together. I want to make you both happy!"

I began to use my hands on David's body to further convince him to stay. I whispered loudly to David, but so Gary could hear, "You have no idea how much I want you both!" David was now reciprocating my touches by groping at my breasts and my ass. I knew they were ready and it was time to move to the bedroom.

I PULLED BACK from our kiss and breathlessly said, "Let's go to the bedroom now. I want you both to make love to me at the same time!" I grabbed both their hands and led them into my room. I turned around at the edge of the king-size bed and gave them both a hungry look and said, "Come here! I am giving my body to you! I want you to use me. I will do anything you want! Anything."

David jumped first, quickly followed by Gary. They tore at my clothes and it didn't take long before they had stripped me naked and physically thrown me on the bed. Gary moved up and traded between kissing me deeply on the mouth and sucking on my big tits. Meanwhile, David went straight for my pussy with his mouth.

My pussy was clean-shaven, and David's lips and tongue were able to move around freely, without obstruction. I was squirming in pleasure from the attention. It wasn't long before David had inserted two of his thick fingers inside my wet pussy and was thrusting hard while continuing to lick. I was issuing quick little screams as David hit just the right places.

I was also coaxing Gary to start undressing for me, so he kneeled on the bed next to my head and unzipped his pants. He reached in and pulled out his large cock and held it in front of my face. I reached up and took it in both hands and admired its size. I lifted my head and hungrily engulfed the head of his cock and began to suck and lick.

Soon I was rhythmically sucking and stroking Gary's massive cock and I would have been happy to stay there forever, but I could sense that David's finger and tongue action was causing an eruption to build deep inside of me. I began to moan, and my body was quivering when I suddenly climaxed on David's face while trying to scream my pleasure with Gary's cock in my mouth. After a minute of convulsions, I went limp, breathing deeply while still grasping Gary in my hand.

Looking down I saw David's smiling face beaming back at me and I said, "That was great, Sweetie! My husband could never make me cum like that! C'mon up here, I want a good look at both of you!" I directed them to both stand by the bed and I helped them both completely undress. Once they had stripped I knelt on the floor in front of them and looked up to admire their bodies.

Gary was taller than David by at least four inches, but with a thinner build, although still athletic. He was lean and well-toned. David was stouter with thick, muscular arms and thighs. They both had sweet faces and big smiles, but David's smile was now rimmed with a shiny wet layer of my pussy juices.

Looking downward to my eye-level I had a good close view of their large cocks. Gary's was nearly eight inches long, relatively thick, light brown and with a wide head. David's impressive member was much, much darker and shorter by only about an inch. It was still plenty long enough for me! What was so impressive though, was its girth. It was so thick that I knew I had never encountered one like it before.

I reached out to touch them and I began to compliment them both. The more I talked, the more the guys swelled with pride. "Oh my God! You have the most beautiful cocks I have ever seen. My girlfriends were right about black cocks being so much bigger and better than white ones!" I reached out with both hands and grasped Gary in my left and David in my right. Although shorter, David's cock felt much heavier in my hand.

I decided to start with Gary and I gave him a quick smile before I leaned forward and wrapped my lips around the head of his cock. "Mmmm! You taste so good!" I said between sucks and licks on his yummy cock. I tried to keep David satisfied with my hand, but it was hard to maintain control over something so big. I figured I had better give him some oral attention soon.

I turned from Gary and looked up at David and with a wicked smile said, "Look at this thick, black cock! I want it now!" I stretched my lips wide and plunged the head of David's cock into my mouth and sucked and licked him noisily. I then tried to push forward, forcing him even deeper into my mouth. I wasn't very successful; his tremendous girth defeated me. But I didn't give up as I feverishly sucked and licked the head and as much of the shaft as I could fit. It must have felt good to him though because I was hearing some loud moans and exclamations wanting more.

I took David's cock out of my mouth and leaned back to admire them both. I started trading kisses and licks back and forth between their cocks and then I smiled up at them and said, "Your cocks feel so good in my mouth! I can't believe that I have two big, black cocks at the same time! My husband's puny little white dick doesn't even fill my mouth. If he could see you both he would be ashamed!"

I pulled both cocks toward me and tried to cram both into my mouth at once. I knew it wasn't going to work, but I had to try it just once. I had to satisfy myself with just kissing and licking them both and rubbing their enormous cocks all over my face. I stopped and looked up at David and I said, "I want you to fuck my mouth with your big, black cock while I jerk off Gary!"

David didn't hesitate, and he positioned himself in front of my face and gently grabbed my head and pulled my mouth onto his cock. He held me firmly as he started thrusting his cock forward and back slowly, but soon he increased his tempo and his thrusts. I was keeping my hand busy on Gary while concentrating on stretching my mouth as wide as possible to fit around David's massive member. I stopped him just long enough to tell him, "I love your cock, David! Tell me what you are going to do to me with it!"

David was a quick learner and he played along with my dirty talk and gave it back to me. As he was thrusting harder and harder into my mouth he said, "Suck my cock, Mya! Take my black cock deep in your mouth. Deeper!" Encouraged, I responded to his words by pushing even more of him into my mouth. He kept going, "You like my black cock in your mouth, I can tell. I'm going to fuck your pussy next! Your husband's dick must be so small that I'm going to have to stretch you out to fit my big cock inside you!"

My pussy was soaking wet from his cock and his nasty talk. I was responding to David with my mouth, with gobs of saliva streaming from my lips and down his shaft, while stroking Gary even harder with my hand. I was surprised at that point to hear Gary pipe up, "Hey, it's my turn! I want to fuck your mouth, Mya! I'm going to push my long, black cock all the way down your throat!"

I was so shocked at Gary's forceful demand that I imme-diately pulled back from David and gave him a wink. I turned and without waiting for an invitation dove onto Gary's cock. I started to stroke David's dripping wet cock with one hand while Gary forcefully grabbed my head and immediately began to thrust into my mouth! I had to fight hard not to gag, but I had become pretty good at deep-throating lately, and since he wasn't as thick as David I could handle a good amount of his total length.

Gary was obviously enjoying the mouth-fuck he was giving me because he closed his eyes and kept thrusting and moaning. I kept this up for quite a while, but I stopped Gary when I thought he was getting too close to climaxing. I wasn't ready to lose one of my partners just yet! I was looking forward to what was yet to come.

I pulled back and began to stroke both of them at once. I smiled up at them and my face and chin were shiny and drip-ping with my spit from the mouth-fucking. I said, "I am so lucky to have met you both tonight! I will always remember your beautiful black cocks, especially when I see my husband's pitiful little shriveled dick. It will bring a smile to my face and he will never suspect a thing!

"But now I need you to fuck me with those big cocks! Get up on the bed now." We all climbed up on the bed and I said, "I think I need to work my way up to David's thick fireplug; Gary fuck me with that long dick of yours!" I pushed David over to a sitting position at the head of the bed and crawled between his legs to suck his cock while I raised my ass for Gary's entry to my dripping wet pussy.

Gary was ready, his cock was still rock hard from the mouth-fuck and he took his position kneeling behind me. I quickly grabbed a tube of lubrication I kept in the bed stand drawer and said, "I'm gonna need this stuff for you two monsters!" Gary grasped his cock and proceeded to slather it up with the lubrication. Once done, he grabbed my ass to steady it and parted my pussy lips with the tip of his cock and pushed forward.

I felt that glorious feeling of initial entry and then it just kept going and going and going! Gary was slowly pushing his full length inside of me, stretching my pussy wide and reaching depths that were rarely touched. The electric shocks I felt in my pussy were shooting up my back, my neck and into the pleasure center of my brain!

I was keeping my mouth and hands mostly busy on David's black beast, but I had to stop several times to cry out, "Oh, shit! Yes! Fuck me with that black cock! Yes!" After another minute of this, I added, "Oh yes, Gary! Fuck me harder! Stretch me out!" Gary was fucking me even harder now, slamming his pelvis into my round ass cheeks, his balls slapping against me with each stroke. I knew that if I let him continue he would soon explode. I had to slow him down yet again.

I said, "Stop Gary, I want you to fuck my asshole now! Only my husband has ever fucked my ass before and his little dick didn't satisfy me. I want your big, black cock inside my ass!" Although this wasn't true, I was sure Gary would like to think it was. I had been fucked in the ass by several of my recent conquests. In fact, most of the guys I had met over the recent months were happy to fuck my nice, round ass.

Gary pulled out of my pussy and conscientiously lubed up his dick again before approaching my asshole. He spread my ass cheeks to expose my pretty little asshole. He went very slowly because he didn't want to hurt me; he was such a sweet guy! He pressed the tip of his cock against my asshole and pushed. It didn't work at first, so he tried again pushing a little harder.

My asshole started to open for him, but I could tell Gary was afraid of hurting me, so he pulled back. I had to plead with him to continue, speaking around the head of David's cock between my lips, "Please, Gary! I want your big cock inside my asshole! I'm ready for it!" Like a trooper, Gary tried again, this time firmly grabbing my hips with both hands and leaning into me, pushing his cock forward until my asshole accepted the head of his cock. He was inside!

∼

I MOANED with pleasure as Gary stretched me out, pushing himself deeper and deeper inside me. He felt great, but I also knew I needed Gary to prepare me for David. I had never had such a thick cock inside my ass as David's, but I had every intention of letting him try. I was planning something else too, but for now, I was happy to enjoy the feel of Gary fucking my ass while I continued to give my oral attention to David's cock and balls.

Gary was now pushing himself fully in and out of my ass while I was busy licking every inch of David's cock. I was so happy at that moment, and from the sounds coming from Gary, I could tell he was too. I knew I would have to change things around again or I would lose Gary too soon. Besides, it was only fair to give David some equal time.

"Gary, honey, let's give David a chance now. Switch places so I can suck on your pretty cock awhile!" I don't think Gary was happy to stop fucking my ass before he climaxed, but David was ready for his turn. Gary pulled away from me and went to the master bathroom to clean himself off a little while David moved around behind me. I said, "David, baby, I need your big, fat cock in my pussy!"

David had already started lubricating his cock in preparation and now he was eagerly moving into position. Gary was simultaneously climbing on the bed in front of me, staying on his knees so that his cock was directly in front of my face. I was just reaching out for it with my hand when David first entered me from behind. I grabbed Gary's cock and cried out, "Oh shit! Yes! Give it to me deeper!"

David didn't wait. He started pushing forward, his thick cock stretching me wide. I had Gary's cock in a death-grip, bracing myself against the onslaught of David's cock in my pussy. I cried out, mostly in pleasure, but with just the right amount of sweet pain, "Oh my God! Yes! Keep going!" David kept pushing until he was fully inside me and then he immediately started to withdraw, preparing to plunge it deeply in again.

David pushed again, harder and, it seemed to me, even deeper. I was just starting to wrap my lips around the head of Gary's cock when David reached the hilt. I cried out again, "Fuck me! Fuck me! Oh my God, your cock feels so good. I love the feel of your thick black cock!" David liked what I was saying because he started to thrust in and out of me harder and faster.

David fucked me for several minutes with long strokes, building slowly in force. The nerves in my pussy were firing sparks. I wanted to stay like this forever with David fucking me from behind while I licked and sucked Gary's long cock, but my body decided it could take no more and I began to convulse with a mighty orgasm. My body shook and quivered as I knelt there impaled by these two large cocks.

Although I had just experienced my second orgasm of the evening I wasn't close to being done, and I knew the guys were ready for more. Gary's cock had felt so good in my ass earlier and now I wanted to see how David's immense cock would feel; if it would even fit. I was about to say so when I felt David pull out of my pussy.

I looked back over my shoulder to see David lubing his dick again and he gave me a wicked smile. He said, "I'm going to fuck your asshole now, Mya. I have wanted to fuck your sweet ass since I first saw you bend over in front of us at the club!" I gave him a wink and a smile and turned my attention back to Gary.

David was now ready and so was I. Thankfully, Gary's cock had loosened me up so that when David's cock first entered my asshole it felt just right. Of course, that was just the tip. Now he started to push forward with his thick shaft. Gary had also become more assertive and he had once again taken ahold of my head and began to fuck my mouth like earlier. I felt his long cock pushing deeper into my throat as David pushed harder from behind, stretching my asshole wide.

My eyes must have been bugging out of my head as I felt these two large cocks pushing deeper inside me, but the guys could only hear my muffled cries as they both began to thrust into me harder and harder. David's fat cock was deep within my ass and I was becoming accustomed to how it felt, stretching my insides. Gary was now so into the moment that he began the nasty talk too. "Oh, Mya! Take my cock deep into your throat! I want to cum inside you!"

David was mostly quiet except for some grunts and moans. Although I couldn't see him I was sure he was getting ready to pump his load of cum inside my ass. Normally I would have loved the thought of accepting the cum of these two men deep within me, one in my mouth and one in my ass, but I had decided that I first wanted to try one more thing, something that I had never tried before.

I MANAGED to pull myself from Gary's long cock enough to tell them, "I'm sorry guys, but I need you to do something for me. My girlfriends have told me about this and now that I have both of you here I need to try it. They tell me it feels so good!" David reluctantly withdrew from my ass and continued to stroke his cock as I pulled Gary down onto the bed so I could crawl on top of him.

Gary was now lying on his back with his long cock sticking straight up. I lowered myself onto him until he was completely inside me. I rode him up and down for several strokes to get things started and then I leaned forward to raise my ass in the air. I could see that David was already catching on and he was smiling, still stroking his thick cock while adding more lubrication, when I said, "Alright, David darling, now put that thick black cock of yours back into my asshole!"

David jumped forward and positioned himself behind me. I imagined that my already loosened asshole was gaping up at him and that's when I felt the head of his cock enter my ass. It was a tight fit before, but with Gary's cock filling my pussy it was getting pretty crowded down there. It took some effort on David's part, and some heavy concentration on mine, but slowly he entered my asshole, pushing forward a little, waiting for my body to acclimate and then pushing again.

I held my breath for most of David's initial insertion, which seemed to take forever, but once he was fully inside I gasped in air deeply and then cried out, "Oh Fuck! Oh God! I've never had two cocks in me at once! My friends were right; it feels wonderful!"

My body was slowly becoming accustomed to having their big cocks filling both my pussy and asshole at once. I wanted to feel more, so I said, "Fuck me now! I want to feel you both fucking me at once!" We started the slow awkward movement of trying to get three bodies moving together in unison. It took some time to work it out.

Gary was pushing his hips up and down as best he could. I tried to help by lifting my ass up and down in opposition to his movement to increase the stroke length of his cock in my pussy. Meanwhile, David was using my limited movements to time his thrusts in and out of my ass. He had the most freedom of movement and was able to penetrate me more easily.

I was overwhelmed by the intense pleasure I was experiencing. My body felt completely filled up and my pussy was buzzing. I couldn't help but cry out, "Oh my God this feels so good. Yes, that's it! Fuck my poor little pussy and asshole!"

The guys were mostly quiet at this point, concentrating on the rhythm of their movements. I wanted to coax them along, so I continued to encourage them, "I can't believe I have two big, black cocks in me at once! You feel so much better than my husband's puny little white dick!"

David and Gary had settled into a groove and were moving in unison. I continued, "Now I know how much better it feels to be fucked by a black cock! My husband should be ashamed to show his tiny little white dick to me, but he'll never know that I have been fucked at once by two black studs!"

They were now moving faster, both building toward a climax so I cried out one more time, "Oh my God! I can't wait for you to cum. I want you to cum inside me!" And then they both did. Gary in my pussy and David in my ass. They came almost at the same time with Gary coming just seconds after David. I felt full but I knew what was about to happen next so I yelled out, "I also want to taste your cum! I want you to come all over me! I want to swallow your sweet, black cum!"

～

BLAM! We all stopped moving, startled by the loud bang, and then, "WHAT THE FUCK IS GOING ON HERE?"

I turned toward the bedroom door and screamed out, "Oh

my God! Zach! What are you doing home?" My husband stood by the open door. He had a look of rage in his face as his eyes darted back and forth between me, Gary and David. Their cocks were still inside me, but I could already feel them softening. The guys were frozen in fear at being caught in the act. I continued, "Zach, I'm sorry! I can explain!"

"Shut up you whore! I suspected you were sleeping around on me, so I decided to check up on you tonight. But I never thought you would stoop to this, and in my own fucking bed!" My husband's face was red, and I could see the veins popping in his neck.

I felt David pull out of me and he started to move to get off the bed while saying, "Listen, man, I'm sorry! We'll just get our stuff and leave."

"The hell you will! Don't any of you move!" We all saw my husband pull a gun from his pocket and point it toward us. "I should just shoot you all now! No jury would convict me for killing two men I caught fucking my wife in my bed!"

Gary's eyes went wide with fright and I'm sure David's did too. They both stopped moving but began to speak out of fear. Gary said, "No, no! You can't do that! We'll just leave! We won't tell anyone about this, we promise!"

Zach moved the gun back and forth. He seemed to be calming down a little, but now he spoke in a quieter, more menacing way, "Oh no, you two aren't going anywhere. I heard you in here, fucking my wife. I was standing outside the door for the last five minutes. I heard that little slut saying how much she liked black cock!"

Zach reached into his other pocket and pulled out his cell phone as he said, "Now don't move a muscle or I'll shoot all of you right now!" We all stayed still as he fumbled with the phone for a second, and then there was a flash of light.

As my eyes recovered from the flash I could see that Zach was pointing the gun toward me. He said, "I heard what you said about me, you little bitch! And I heard you say that you want to swallow their cum!" He waved the gun toward David and Gary as he continued to speak to me, "So now I'm going to divorce your pretty little ass and take everything you've got. This picture will ensure that I can't lose. You've done me a favor; I was hoping to dump your ass, but now I can do that and take your money too!"

I cried out, "Zach! Please don't! I'm sorry!" I started to cry.

Zach just started to laugh and said, "It's too late for that you cheating slut! But I don't want you to go away without anything; so, before I kick you out with nothing I'm going to let you have your little wish. These two fine gentlemen are going to oblige by cumming in your mouth and I'm going to stand right here and watch you swallow their black cum!"

"What?" I cried. "Are you nuts?"

David said, "No way, man! We can't do that. We're just going to leave." Gary was nodding along with David.

Zach lowered the gun toward David and said, "That's too bad. Then I guess I'm just going to have to kill all of you right now. I've already figured out what to tell the police; how I came home and heard my wife screaming that she was being raped. I tried to stop the two guys, but in my panicked state, I accidentally shot her too. Either that or the jealous husband story. Either way, you'll all be dead."

David and Gary just sat there stunned. Zach continued, "Or you can do what I tell you and then walk away. As much as I would love to shoot you both for fucking my wife, I owe you my thanks. Because of you, I can dump her sorry little ass. So, what's it gonna be, boys? Are you going to give my lovely wife her final wish or do I shoot you now?"

Gary replied this time, "Man, I don't want you to shoot us, but I don't think I can do what you're asking with you sitting there pointing a gun at us!"

Zach just grinned back and said, "You just came inside her

and you were ready to cum all over her just a few minutes ago. You had better figure out how to finish the job now or it'll be the last time you use that big pecker of yours!"

I stepped in then. "Don't shoot, Zach! It's not their fault; it's mine. We'll do what you want." I moved off the bed and looked at David and Gary and said, "I'm sorry guys for getting you into this! Let's get this over with so you can leave." I got down on my knees and motioned them to come over and stand in front of me. They moved off the bed and stood next to each other in front of me. Zach moved around to lean against the dresser so he could have a clear view.

THE BOYS LOOKED nervous and fidgety as I reached out for their cocks. They weren't the same big stiff cocks that had been fucking me earlier. They were hanging much limper. I looked up at David and Gary and quietly said, "Forget about him. Close your eyes and just concentrate on me. We can do this together." I grasped their cocks and began to stroke them as they closed their eyes.

I was doing my best to bring their big cocks back to life. I started with my hands and then began to use my mouth. In between, I would softly say encouraging things to them, "Yes, that's it. Your cock tastes so good, baby. Mmmm, I love the way it feels!" The boys kept their eyes closed, but I kept looking over toward Zach. He was watching intently as I pleasured the two black men, a large smile on his face.

I was affecting both guys, but it was taking a long time. I kept up the soft encouragement and my mouth stimulation. Zach said, "Don't forget to tell them how much you prefer their black cocks to mine, my sweet!"

I felt the boys cringe at the sound of Zach's voice invading the little space I was trying to build around them, space where it was only them and me. I quickly said, "Shut up, Zach! You're not helping!"

Zach huskily whispered, "That's fine. I'll be quiet, but you were so happy to say those things before that I want you to say them now in front of me. Go on, do it!"

I gave Zach a sideways glance and saw his big, leering smile. I returned my attention to David and Gary, but I followed Zach's demand. While sucking on both their cocks, moving back and forth between them, I quietly talked to them to encourage them toward a climax. "Your black cocks are so big and so sweet! I loved feeling you inside me. I love big, black cocks and yours are the best!"

After several more minutes, this seemed to work. They were getting hard again. I kept this up for longer, exerting more pressure and increasing my speed. I could now see the guys starting to twitch and stiffen their bodies a little. I knew it wouldn't be much longer.

Gary was the first to near the finish line. That's when he grabbed his cock and started to masturbate himself. His eyes remained closed and his face was scrunched in concentration, probably willing himself to get this over with. I kept my mouth on David's thick cock, while Gary kept on stroking himself, occasionally pausing to give Gary some encouragement, "That's it, baby! Cum for me! I want to taste your sweet cum in my mouth!"

Several times tonight Gary had been near the peak and I had stopped him each time. Even though he had finally shot a load into my pussy right before all this, he had built up quite a pent-up load and he exhaled now as he released it directly into my waiting lips. His first shot was forceful and voluminous. Most of it went into my mouth, but some of it splashed off my lips and teeth and fell onto my chin and dripped down onto my tits. There were several more volleys of his cum to follow of lesser and lesser amounts, but the total amount was indeed huge. Much of it was plastered all over my face.

As soon as Gary had started to ejaculate, and my attention had turned toward him, David had grabbed his thick cock and began to stroke it madly. He too was anxious to end this ordeal and he was still working on it now. I could see he was on the verge of his orgasm. With my open mouth still full of Gary's cum I turned to look at Zach. He raised his hand as if to give me a silent signal not to swallow yet.

I heard a small moan come from David's lips and I turned back toward him and his hand stroking his large cock directly in front of me. I couldn't whisper anything to him with my mouth full of Gary's cum, but I did try to give him encouraging moans and sounds.

Suddenly David's eyes opened wide and he looked down at me as he gave out a loud guttural sound. He positioned the head of his cock directly over my mouth just as he started to cum. David's ejaculation wasn't as forceful as Gary's, but it was just as voluminous. His semen spilled out of his thick cock and straight down into my mouth and onto my face. David kept up a constant moan as he stroked his cock multiple more times while milking every last drop of cum onto me.

SUDDENLY IT WAS QUIET. David and Gary were standing there. We all looked over at Zach who still had that leering grin on his face, seemingly happy at what he had forced us to do, the gun still trained on us. I had closed my mouth but had not yet swallowed. My face was covered with a large amount of semen. I gave Zach a "What now?" look.

He said, "You know, I enjoyed that. Open your mouth sweetie, show me what these nice boys gave you." I complied and tilted back my head and opened my mouth wide to show Zach the huge amount of cum in there.

Zach said, "You are quite the little slut aren't you, Mya? Well, you said that you wanted to swallow their black cum, go ahead. That's the last wish of yours that I will grant you!"

Zach was looking me directly in the eyes as he spoke, and I was staring right back at him, defiantly. For that moment it was almost like we were the only two beings in the world. I maintained my gaze as I slowly closed my mouth. I flicked a little smile up at him from the corners of my mouth and then I proceeded to swallow Gary and David's cum!

Zach didn't say a word for several moments as he looked down at me on my knees, but then he seemed to wake up from his trance. He pointed the gun at Gary and David and said, "Alright, you two have had your fun for the night. Grab your clothes and get the hell out of my house before I change my mind!"

Gary and David scrambled to put their clothes on and they started to leave the room, but Gary stopped and said, "What are you going to do to Mya?" I smiled a little; I knew Gary had a kind heart. I felt a pang of sorrow.

Zach growled, "Don't worry, Don Juan. I'm not going to hurt her. She's my meal ticket, remember? Unless I find out you two go talking to anyone about this, then she might get hurt! And you too! Don't forget, I've still got that picture. Now get out of here!"

Gary and David gave me a quick look of helplessness. I gave them a small smile back and nodded that it was okay for them to leave. They bolted from the room and I heard the front door open and then slam shut.

I REMAINED on my knees on the floor while Zach moved over

to the window to see if the guys had left before he turned back to me. He moved closer and said, "And as for you, my pretty little slut..."

I looked up into Zach's face as he continued, "You were fantastic, Mya!"

I smiled. It had been one hell of a night! Zach helped me up. He was so excited that he just kept talking a mile a minute, "That was the best one yet. I can't believe you brought two guys home! We talked about it, but I didn't think we'd ever get that lucky!"

I replied, "Yeah. I'll admit I was a little nervous about that. What if they came over all heroic and jumped you? What would they have done once they found out the gun is fake?"

Zach was now walking into the bathroom as he called back over his shoulder, "They would have kicked my ass is what they would have done."

He came back out bringing me a damp washcloth so I could clean their drying cum from my face. "So," I asked, "Did we get it all?"

"Absolutely!" Zach exclaimed. "We've got the three fixed video cameras catching the bedroom action from all sides, and I was able to use the hidden zoom camera for some good close-up shots. I got some great footage of you sucking the tall guy's cock, and I also got some good footage when the big guy was fucking your ass! The look on your face was priceless!" I smiled at the memory.

Zach said, "And the double penetration! Mya, that was beautiful! I just about blew my load watching that on the monitor from the other room. It took all my willpower not to grab my cock and jerk off right then. I had to bite my tongue to keep from making noise too soon and messing up the whole thing. As it was, I was afraid I would have a visible erection when I ran into the room to confront them!"

I looked down at Zach's crotch now and could clearly see

his large erection because he was so excited by what we had pulled off tonight, and what was yet to come. That was one of my biggest lies of the night to Gary and David; Zach's cock isn't puny at all. It is big. Not as big as theirs, maybe, but he knows how to use it.

Zach smiled and said, "Why don't you go take a quick shower while I set up the video player. Hurry back! By the time we get to the part where the big guy is fucking you, I plan to be balls deep in your ass!"

I headed for the shower thinking, "Yeah, my husband has driven me to this, and I'm glad. Our sex life is amazing, and tonight he will be getting what he deserves!"

THE END

Get Access to over 20 more FREE Erotica Downloads at Shameless Book Deals

Shameless Book Deals is a website that shamelessly brings you the very best erotica at the best prices from the best authors to your inbox every day. Sign up to our newsletter to get access to the daily deals and the Shameless Free Story Archive!

A NEIGHBOR IN NEED BY SHARRA SOMERS

From the outside, Wendy and Charles had a perfect marriage, but Charles didn't seem to be enough to satisfy his wife. When Charles asks his beefy black neighbor to help his wife around the house, they all get more than they bargained for.

~

*W*endy sat at the window and watched her husband pull out of the driveway. Charles was a good man and a wonderful provider. He was someone she had been proud to introduce to her parents when they had first started dating, and they matched one another well in almost every way, to the point that her friends had started calling them Barbie and Ken. In most ways, Charles was the perfect husband. Despite all of these things, Wendy shifted her eyes to their bedroom door and frowned. Even though they were a great couple in most areas, Charles never seemed to be able to satisfy her in the bedroom. It had gotten to the point that he wasn't even hugging her when he came home at night, probably because he didn't want to get her hopes up. Wendy tried to push away her frustration, but she couldn't help feeling neglected and ignored.

For just a moment she had gotten her hopes up this morning. She woke up to Charles spooning her, his erection pressed against her backside and his hands exploring her body. When his fingertips swept over her nipples, she had arched into him and ground her ass against his cock. She felt his breathing deepen, and he growled into her blonde hair. Wendy had shifted her hips and parted her legs to encourage Charles to enter her, but his cock didn't seem to be long enough for the angle. He had tugged at her to pull her onto him, and she had straddled him, gasping when he entered her. She had ridden him while he massaged her breasts, and she had just started building to an orgasm when it was over. Charles came and pulled her down beside him, hugging her briefly before getting up and heading to the shower to get ready for work. At the time, Wendy hadn't known whether to be angry or hurt. Now she just felt hopeless.

Well, he isn't here now. Maybe I should spend time taking care of myself. Wendy had always felt awkward trying to pleasure herself, but maybe today she could focus on herself. Wendy went to the bathroom and started the tub running and drizzled bath oil into the warm water. A few minutes later, Wendy slid into the water and inhaled the lavender scent rising from the steam. She closed her eyes and ran her hands over her stomach and to her breasts, trying to recapture those initial sensations from the morning. At first, it was hard to get past how she'd felt when Charles had just gotten up and left her. He hadn't even kissed her before he left for work! But she kept thinking about what it had felt like when she had first woken up, the way his cock felt against her, the feel of his fingers on her skin as they moved up her stomach to her tits. This time she lingered on her nipples the way she had wanted Charles to do, stroking and pinching them. Wendy drizzled more oil on her nipples, and she felt a rush of pleasure as she swirled her fingertips in the oil and massaged it into the hard buds. She moaned at the sensation, and she ran her tongue over her lips and imagined someone suckling her nipples. One of her hands massaged her breast and teased at the nipple as the other hand drifted downward toward her sex. Just as Wendy was parting her legs to give herself access, she heard a loud knock on the front door.

The morning's frustration returned with a vengeance. For a moment, Wendy considered ignoring the intrusion, but she bolted out of the water at the sound of a second knock. Grabbing the towel, she did a quick dry off before grabbing her silk bathrobe and heading toward the door. She was tying the knot as she jerked open the door.

"Yes?!" She knew she sounded irritated, so she tried to force herself to smile when she saw her neighbor, Kris Copeland, on the other side of the door. Kris's skin was as dark as Wendy's was white. He stood just over six feet tall, and Wendy was getting an eyeful. Normally she saw him in a black business suit, but today he was in a tank top and shorts that didn't leave much to the imagination. His dark skin seemed to accentuate his smile, but Wendy's eyes drifted to his broad shoulders, down his tight waist to the bulge between his legs. Her eyes snapped back to meet his.

Kris's smile had broadened, and Wendy hoped he hadn't realized how much attention she had given to his physique. She then realized she was giving him just as much of an eyeful. She was still damp, and the silk clung to her skin. She felt herself blushing under his gaze.

"Hi, Kris! How are you doing?" She hoped her voice didn't sound as sexed up as she felt.

"Hi, Wendy. I hope I didn't interrupt anything." Wendy tried to ignore the possible innuendo in his words. When she shook her head, he continued, "You know Charles helped me with my tax forms last month, and I told him to call me if I could help him out in any way. He called a few minutes ago and told me he thought you had a few things I could help with."

Wendy froze, and she felt her blush deepen. *What the hell is he talking about?!* The only thing Wendy could think of was something she couldn't imagine Charles suggesting, and she was afraid that Kris might know where her mind had gone. If so, he gave no indication that he knew she was thinking about sex. He just stood outside, patiently waiting for her answer.

"Uh, well, why don't you come in and let me think about what he might have meant?" She stepped aside and motioned for him to enter. Kris stepped into the foyer and waited for Wendy to indicate where he should go. Trying to ignore the way he was making her feel, Wendy closed the door and led him into the kitchen. She knew she should know what Charles was talking about, but all she could think about was how much she wanted his hands on her. Pushing that thought away, Wendy glanced around the kitchen.

"Maybe he meant the garbage disposal? It's been making a weird sound, and I mentioned that we should probably call someone out. But, Kris, I don't want to be a bother, especially on a workday."

Kris smiled. "Wendy, I'm taking a week off work just to get away and take care of me. I don't mind helping you out." His voice seemed to deepen, and Wendy felt like he wasn't talking about the garbage disposal. "Sometimes we get so busy with the day-to-day grind that we forget about our own needs and how important they are. Have you ever felt that way?" As he spoke, it seemed like electricity was sparking between them.

Wendy gulped and just nodded as she looked up into

Kris's eyes. She knew that her nipples were hard, and she could feel herself pulsing in desire. It had never occurred to her to step outside of her marriage, but she had never felt this type of sexual energy from anyone before. Her lips felt dry, so Wendy ran her tongue over them reflexively. Kris's eyes didn't miss the movement.

"Are you sure that it's the garbage disposal that needs help?"

Wendy's heart stopped. "What are you thinking?"

"I'm thinking that your husband is away a lot of the time. You're a beautiful woman, in this house by yourself most of the time. I'm wondering if you're getting your needs met." Kris stepped closer, standing so close Wendy was certain she could feel his heat warming her the way the water had earlier. When she didn't answer, Kris leaned down and kissed her.

The kiss started soft, but when Wendy didn't object, Kris wrapped one arm around her waist and pulled her into him and his rock-hard erection. Kris pressed his lips against hers, nipping at her lips and forcing his tongue between her teeth. Wendy moaned and went limp against his onslaught. Kris didn't hesitate. Without breaking the kiss, Kris scooped her into his arms, taking her to the bedroom, kicking off his shoes along the way. When he settled her on the bed, Kris tugged at the loose knot that held Wendy's bathrobe, exposing her to his hungry eyes. Wendy blushed and started to cover herself, but Kris swatted away her hands.

"Oh, no you don't. I want to see what I've been missing. I've wanted this from the first time I saw you." Kris scooped up Wendy's right breast, his black hands seeming even darker against the white of her skin. Kris lowered his head to her breast and suckled, nipping at the hard bud as his hand massaged the other breast. Wendy moaned at the attention and gasped in surprise when he cupped her between her legs.

"Spread them for me. I'm going to wear your ass out!" Wendy blushed but did as he said. She hissed in pleasure when he slid his fingers along her slit, trailing the slick wetness from her cunt to her clit before massaging that bud while starting to suck her nipple again. Wendy felt an orgasm building again, and she prayed to the universe that nothing would stop it this time. Kris seemed to know exactly how to touch her, firm without being too rough with the tender and needy kernel between her legs. Wendy's breathing became more rapid, and she moaned as she rocked against Kris's hand. Her legs started to quiver as the pleasure built inside her. The power of her release slammed through her, and she clamped down on Kris's hand as she rode the pulsing wave of pleasure.

Kris didn't give her time to recover before he slid between her legs to lap at her juices. His tongue entered her, fucking her as he sucked her juices, pausing just long enough to move upward and flick his tongue across her clit before moving back down to tongue fuck her again. Wendy widened her legs and moaned as he drank from her core. She started pumping in time with his mouth, fucking his face, grinding into him, and begging him for more.

"Oh, God! Kris! Please fuck me!" Kris chuckled but kept working her over with his mouth and hands. When Wendy came, her legs went to jelly, and she collapsed, trying to catch her breath, but she tugged at his tank top, urging him to get undressed. This time, Kris complied. He stood up and made sure he had her full attention when he stripped off his tank top and then his shorts.

Wendy's eyes widened at his physique. His body was perfect, sculpted without being huge. Looking at the bulge hidden by Kris's boxers, Wendy could tell she was going to find something monstrous there. Kris let Wendy take in the view before moving his hands to the waistband of his boxers to slide them down his legs. When Kris's black cock popped free, Wendy gaped at its size. *My God! How the hell am I supposed to handle that?!* Drawing a deep breath, Wendy rose onto her hands and knees and stalked toward it. Stopping wasn't an option, so she might as well dive in even though she was afraid he was too much for her. Paraphrasing a statement about eating an elephant, Wendy thought to herself, *How do you suck a giant's cock? One inch at a time.* Biting her lip and smiling up at Kris, Wendy lifted her chin and opened her mouth to take in the first inch. Running her tongue along the slope of his head, Wendy suckled gently, sucking at the cleft and tasting the salty tanginess of Kris's cock. She heard him moan, so she lapped and sucked, alternating pressure and speed as she explored his cock. Wendy swallowed to moisten her throat before she slid another inch downward, teasing the vein that ran down the length of his cock. With the other hand she massaged the base of his shaft while her mouth worked up and down the first two inches of his rock-hard cock. She heard Kris moan at the attention, and she felt him shudder as he started rocking against her face.

Wendy swallowed another inch of cock and then pulled back up to suckle his head before reversing down him again. She kept alternating the motions while listening to Kris's breathing. It had gotten ragged, and Wendy could taste the tanginess of his pre-cum. She didn't want to stop, but she also wanted to be fucked, so on her next upstroke, Wendy pulled back, kissed the tip, and tried to pull away.

"Oh, no you don't. We're going to finish this." Kris's black hands pressed into Wendy's blonde hair and pushed her head back to his cock. Wendy complied and opened up for him. When she slid down his shaft, sucking and licking all the way, Kris moaned and started rocking against her. Wendy began flicking her tongue side to side to tease him more. She slipped her hand down to cup his balls, and she gently massaged them as she sucked harder and rode up and down his shaft. She took more of him into her with each down-stroke, but Wendy knew there was no way she was going to be able to take all of him into her throat. *Hell, I'm not sure I can take all of him into my pussy!*

Kris kept pumping as Wendy swallowed to pull more of him into her. Just when she thought she was going to suffo-cate, she heard him roar out and she tasted his release as it flooded into her. Wendy swallowed as fast as she could, drinking down everything he pumped into her. When his cock finally emptied itself, Wendy gently sucked it clean. Kris moaned and collapsed against her on the bed.

Wendy felt disappointed that he had finished before fucking her, but her disappointment lasted only a few minutes. Kris leaned into her, kissing her in a way that let her know he was not finished with her yet, despite his orgasm. As their kiss continued, Wendy felt his cock hard-ening again. Kris must have seen the shock on her face because he laughed.

"Not used to a man able to keep going?" Wendy just shook her head in amazement. Kris smiled broadly for a moment, then his look became predatory. Wendy gulped as he grabbed her pussy and drove two fingers inside of her. Her sex was ready for him, but she wasn't used to the forceful approach he was taking. *Wendy, you're not really used to sex at all.* Charles had been her first and only, and she was quickly learning how much she didn't know.

Kris worked her pussy with his fingers and watched the white woman writhe in pleasure. After a bit, he pulled his fingers from her and sniffed her scent before licking her juices from his fingers and then lunging at her and forcing her knees apart. Kris drove inside of her, and Wendy cried out from pleasure and pain as he seemed to tear her apart. She moaned as he pulled out and cried out again when he slammed back into her. Wendy felt her body stretching as it tried to accommodate him, but she thought she was going to rip apart before she took him all in.

"Damn, you so tight you feel like a virgin! You ever get dick?"

Wendy had clamped her eyes shut but she shook her head. "No, not like this. Oh, God!" She lifted her hips to try to open up more for him, and she felt her juices flowing. Part of her wondered if some of it might be blood. Despite the pain, Wendy felt another sort of pressure building inside her and she knew she was going to cum. Her moaning got louder, and she started rocking her hips in time with Kris. He started grinding his hips as he thrust into her, and he hit something deep inside her. Wendy screamed as the orgasm ripped through her, and she collapsed from a kind of pleasure she had never felt before.

When she came to, it took Wendy a moment to figure out where she was. *Ok. I'm in my bedroom. I'm naked. And Kris... Oh, right.* Wendy blushed again as she looked at this black god lying next to her. He flashed her a self-satisfied grin.

"You ok?" Kris looked like he knew the answer. Wendy nodded.

"Um, yes. I just...well, I'm still sorting everything out." Now it was Kris's turn to nod.

"It's been a big day. I'm glad Charles saw me this morning when he was heading out to work."

Wendy winced at her husband's name. She had never even thought about adultery—she had always felt weird even when she was masturbating, but here she was in bed with one of her husband's friends. Wendy knew she should probably tell Kris to go and that they could never do anything like this again, but looking at him, she didn't want this to stop. She looked up to meet Kris's eyes and then shifted them down to his penis, which was still ready for more. Even though she knew she shouldn't continue, she slid down and took Kris back into her mouth.

She tasted her own juices as she suckled, and she felt herself getting turned on even more. Kris made her feel freer than she had ever felt, like her needs mattered. Wendy slid down his shaft, licking and sucking.

"Touch yourself while you do that." Kris's voice was deep and had a low growl to it. Wendy blushed but she complied. She opened her legs and smeared her juices up to her clit. When she stroked it, electricity shot through her body, and she moaned. She froze and savored the feeling. She had never felt like this with Charles, and she never would have allowed herself to do these things with him. He was just…too white bread for this sort of thing.

"Keep moving." Kris's voice was primal, anything but white bread. Wendy obeyed, sucking his cock while circling and teasing her clit. It felt so good that it was hard for her to focus on her duties. Soon, Kris tugged at her, pulling her back into his beefy, black arms. He planted a hard kiss on her lips, and then flipped her around like she weighed nothing. Wendy found her face back at his crotch, but this time she was positioned to give Kris access to her core. Wendy opened her mouth to continue sucking Kris's cock, and Kris began lapping at Wendy's clit. Wendy slid up and down his cock while pressure built again inside of her. Kris felt Wendy begin quivering, so he began pumping his cock in time with the work his mouth was doing. When Wendy orgasmed, he shifted them again, putting her on hands and knees facing the garden window. This time he didn't give her time to recover but slammed into her from behind, driving into her. Wendy's arms gave underneath her, and her face planted onto the mattress, but she pumped up to meet his thrusts. Arching her back like a cat, Wendy felt more alive than she had ever been. Kris drove his black cock deeper inside her, and she could hear him moaning.

"Your man can't fuck you like this, can he? He can't satisfy you like I can."

"No. God, no."

"Tell me how much you want my black cock."

"I want it. God, keep giving it to me." Wendy was practically crying from the pleasure. She looked down between her legs and saw him slapping against her ass as he drove into her. Raising her head, she looked through the window and froze. Standing outside, almost hidden by the hydrangeas was Charles staring at what was happening in his bed. Wendy tried to twist away from Kris, but his hold on her hips was too strong.

"Kris, wait! It's…" And then Wendy realized something else. Charles was holding his cock and was pumping it in time with the black man's thrusts.

"Show him what it's like to be fucked by a MAN. Show him what you've been needing. What he can't give you." Kris's voice was loud—loud enough for Charles to hear. Wendy thought her husband looked ashamed, but he kept working his cock. Wendy decided to obey.

"Oh, baby, let me taste you! Show me how much dick you have for me!"

Kris pulled out, inch by inch, and pointed to the floor in front of the window. "Kneel for me then."

Wendy complied, kneeling in front of the window where Charles stood. She didn't look at her husband again but kept her focus completely on the black man before her. His cock stood at attention inches from her mouth.

"Tell me how much you want this. Tell me how much you need this."

Wendy did. "I want you. I need your cock. I need your *black cock.*" Wendy knew they were putting on a show for her husband, but she meant every word of what she was saying. She did need Kris's black cock.

"Tell me how much better it is than your husband's." Wendy didn't want to hurt Charles, but she thought it was obvious how much more Kris had to offer.

"Kris, your cock is the best I've had. It's so huge!"

Kris nodded, and Wendy started sucking him as if she were starving for it. She moaned at the taste and savored the way it felt in her mouth. She opened wider and slid down even further than before. When Kris pushed the back of her head, she continued bobbing to take all of him down her throat. This time, when she tasted his pre-cum, Kris pulled out.

"Turn around." Staying on her knees, Wendy complied.

"Get down like a dog." Wendy felt herself pulsing in anticipation, but she also wondered what Charles was doing. Glancing to the side, she could see that he had shifted to get a better view. Smiling, she widened her stance to give Kris better access and her husband a better view. She heard Kris chuckle.

"That's right. Open for me. Beg me for it."

Wendy wanted it so bad that she didn't have to act. "Oh, God! Fuck me. Please, God. Fuck me!"

Kris slammed into her and drove Wendy to the carpet. He braced himself with one hand on her back and ground into her as he pumped even harder than before. Wendy cried in pleasure and pain but begged him to keep going, to fuck her. She rocked her hips trying to push him even more. She could hear Kris's breathing becoming louder, and she felt her own orgasm building.

"Oh, God! Kris! I'm going to cum!" Kris kept pounding into her. She started tightening and relaxing her muscles, trying to push them both over the edge. Her orgasm hit first, but she kept working her muscles, and when he roared from his release, she milked him dry. Kris collapsed onto her, his black body covering her like a blanket and his monstrous cock still quivering inside her.

They lay together for several minutes. When Kris shifted, his cock slipped out, and Wendy started to get up. Kris grabbed her waist. "Where are you going?"

Wendy smiled. Charles rarely wanted to stay wrapped up after sex. "Don't worry. I just want to take care of you." Wendy slid down and took his cock in her hands before leaning down and lapping it clean. Kris squirmed at the sensation, and Wendy smiled. "I know. It's tender." She settled back into Kris's arms, and he drew her tight against him. She wondered if Charles was still watching, but she couldn't tell from where she lay. She had no idea what this afternoon would be like. Would Charles pretend nothing had happened? Was he going to file for divorce? Was he going to suggest more of this sort of thing? Wendy had no idea. She also wasn't sure what Kris was thinking.

"Kris?"

"Uh-huh."

"Are we going to keep doing this?" Wendy heard Kris chuckle.

"As far as I'm concerned, every damn chance I get." Wendy felt relief flood her. She loved her husband and didn't want to lose the good things they had. But she was also through with celibacy. Maybe this was a way for everything to work out.

"Kris, did you and Charles have an arrangement?"

"What, for this to happen? No, but I think he must have planned it. I mean, he didn't bust in here and try to break it up. And he seemed to be enjoying the show."

Wendy blushed. "Yes. I saw that." She thought about this morning and how Charles had left her unsatisfied. The fact that he had even initiated sex was strange. *And he hadn't told Kris what I needed from him. Maybe he had planned this out.*

Wendy shifted her attention back to her lover. She lay in Kris's arms thinking about their morning together. "Kris?"

"Yeah?"

"Have you had a vasectomy?" Wendy held her breath.

"No...I never wanted to be walking around shooting blanks. Why? You're on the pill or something, right?"

Wendy's heart stopped beating. "No. Charles and I knew that we didn't want kids, so he had a vasectomy. Not that there was much sex going on." This time it was Kris's turn to freeze. After a moment he shrugged.

"Ok. That's something to sort out if it becomes a problem." Kris smiled again. "But you might want to think about the pill if we're going to keep doing this. And now that we've got a taste of it, I don't think either one of us wants this to stop." He leaned down and kissed her, as slow and as sensual as he had been hard and rough earlier. He teased at her with his tongue and sucked gently on her bottom lip. When her tongue met his, Wendy felt him smile.

"Why don't we move this back up to the bed? We're going to have carpet burns all over us if we stay down here much longer." Kris stood and reached down to pull Wendy into his arms before settling both of them onto the bed. Wendy curled against him, and Kris wrapped his arms around her tiny white waist. She could tell by the why he nuzzled her neck that their day was far from over. As he stroked her side, Wendy felt a rush of heat inside her and knew that she was going to ride his black cock every chance she got. One way or another, she was never going to be sexually frustrated again.

THE END

Get Access to over 20 more FREE Erotica Downloads at Shameless Book Deals

Shameless Book Deals is a website that shamelessly brings you the very best erotica at the best prices from the best authors to your inbox every day. Sign up to our newsletter to get access to the daily deals and the Shameless Free Story Archive!

DARING THE PROFESSOR BY
CHARLOTTE STORM

When a game of Truth or Dare goes too far…
Truth or Dare is a game that should stay at frat parties. How was college Freshman, Kaira Burke, supposed to know her best friend would drag it out all semester? When Kaira learns the truth about her cheating boyfriend, she decides to push the next dare too far. A kiss from her history professor should teach her boyfriend a lesson. But she's not sure she could seduce her professor if she wanted to. She's white. He's black and much much older. Why would he ever be interested in her?

Little does she know the professor wants to teach Kaira a lesson not in the history books. A lesson her boyfriend gets to watch and learn as well.

Daring The Professor is an older male, younger female interracial cuckold that'll dare you to be bold and leave you soaking wet!

～

"*Y*our turn, Burke. Truth or dare?" Mitzi's dark brown eyes gleam underneath the harsh glow of fluorescent lighting. Why our dorm building insists on keeping the study lounge so brightly lit is something I'll never understand.

My best friend and roommate stares at me, waiting for an answer. I roll my eyes. I was over this game when it started a month ago, at a rush week frat party. My boyfriend pledged. That's how we got invited.

Someone suggested we play the ice-breaker game, so we did. Only, Mitzi never stopped playing. She's like a dog with a bone. Always has been. We've been besties since grade school. We even applied to the same college so we could be together. I don't know what I'd do without her. Also, I want to wring her neck sometimes.

"Ugh, not this again," I say, barely glancing up from my computer. I have an essay due tomorrow in English, and I am far from done.

"Yes, this again. I'm *bored*." She throws an M&M at me, which says a lot. Mitzi isn't one to waste food, and I'm pretty sure the bag in her hands is her breakfast.

I nod at her Econ and American History books. "You could always do your homework." *Like I'm trying to do mine.*

She retrieves her thrown M&M all while making a guttural noise that sounds like a cat trying to cough up a semester's worth of missed assignments. "As I said, I'm *bored*. B-O-W-R-E-D!"

I stifle a laugh. "That isn't how you spell it."

She pops a candy-coated chocolatey piece of deliciousness into her mouth. "Just making sure you're paying attention to me and not your essay."

With a heavy sigh, I close my laptop. It's pointless, me

trying to get any work done around her. "I'm paying attention."

"Truth or dare," she repeats. I hate it when she's insistent like this.

I scrub my hands over my face. "I don't want to play, Mitz."

"I dare you to pick dare," she says, a dangerous smirk distorting her features. "I double-dog dare you."

"Then I'm definitely picking truth," I scoff. No double-dog dare ever ended with something benign. There's no way I'm letting her get me into trouble. Not when I'm here on scholarship.

Mitzi sticks out her lower lip and crosses her arms underneath perky tits. Hers are larger than mine by a cup size. Fine by me. She can have the extra. It seems like more to carry around. Nick's never complained about my C-cup.

No, where I envy Mitzi is in her curves and the sultry dark color of her skin. I'm too pale, too blonde and blue-eyed to be interesting. Average everyday white girl, she calls me. She isn't wrong. Nick says he likes me exactly as I am, but he's the same as me. All I've ever had is vanilla. How do I know if I'll like any other flavors?

Mitzi taps her lips with her finger. "Truth. Truth. Hmm... let me see."

While she's trying to figure out a question that will no doubt reveal my darkest secrets, I glance at my phone. We have ten minutes before we need to leave for our History class.

It's easily my favorite class. Not because of the subject matter, but because of Professor Evans. Tall, dark, and handsome as sin, I feel guilty every time I step foot into his class. I can't stop staring at his ass. At his gorgeously dark flesh. At the way his button-down shirt hugs buff arms and a broad chest.

For an older man, he's *hot*. And different. So much more different than I'm used to. Older, wiser, more experienced. *Not* white. It's just a fantasy, though; me imagining what someone like him would be like in bed. Or on a desk in his office. Or in the classroom when no one's there.

I imagine how his biceps would bulge when he grabs my hips from behind. The way he'd grunt when sliding his thick black cock into my tight pink pussy. The thrill of getting caught, especially when I add Nick to the fantasy. Him walking in on us and not getting mad but watching. Maybe joining in.

My dampening panties tell me I've gone too far. It's never going to happen. Professor Evans isn't interested in me. It doesn't matter that I've caught his gaze lingering longer than it should, in places that it shouldn't. And I love Nick. He wouldn't cheat on me. I wouldn't cheat on him. We've been together since high school. Neither of us has any intention of changing that.

"Okay, I've got it." Mitzi sits on the edge of the couch and leans in. "Tell me a secret you'd never want your parents to find out."

I fight the urge to roll my eyes. It isn't that I don't have secrets I wouldn't want my parents to know. It's that Mitzi's been there to help me *make* those secrets. We've always been together, two peas in our own little messed up pod. My boyfriend, Nick, can't quite understand—

My back stiffens and my eyes bulge when I think of the one thing Mitzi doesn't know. No one knows, because it technically hasn't happened yet. It's a gut feeling more than anything. Women's intuition.

"*Gurl.*" She draws out the word. "I can see it all over your face. This is a good one." She glances over her shoulder, leans in close. "You better tell me."

I copy her movements, make sure no one is close enough

to overhear. "Nick's going to propose to me, and I'm going to say yes."

Mitzi's face goes on a serious journey, picking up speed like an out of control train about to run out of track. Shock. Surprise. Doubt. Concern for my sanity. Humor. Fear. Hurt. And finally, resignation. I'm exhausted just staring at her.

Does she think I'm crazy? Probably. Too young? Definitely. But I overheard Nick talking to someone on the phone about marriage. Granted, I'd only heard a tiny bit of the conversation, but the parts I did hear were enough.

"I know we're young," I defend in anticipation of where Mitzi might take this. "And maybe it's a terrible idea. I know the stats are against us, but he loves me. When I'm with him, things are intense. I think we could do this."

Mitzi stares at me, speechless. She falls back, lets the couch hold her up. Her entire body sags as if weighed down by some unseen force. I lean forward, edge of my seat style, and reach for her hand. She doesn't resist when I take it. She doesn't do anything but stare.

"Don't worry," I say, putting as much reassurance as I can into my tone. "This won't change anything. You're still my best friend. I still love you. We can still be old cat ladies together."

She blinks once. Twice. As if she's coming out of a trance. "My—" She clears her throat, tries again. "My turn. Truth," she says before I can ask the question.

"Mitz, we don't have to—"

She squeezes my hand still in hers and looks like she's about to cry when she says, "Nick's been cheating on you."

I DON'T REMEMBER the walk to class or how we got from the dorm lounge to outside. Everything is numb.

This must be what shock feels like.

Mitzi nudges my arm. I'm vaguely aware of Professor Evans giving us instructions. Students stand, move their chairs, get into groups. Mitzi grabs my arm. "You okay, Kaira?"

No. I'm not okay. Not even close. She just dropped the truth bomb about Nick cheating on me with some chick he just met at one of his frat parties. Not only is he not going to propose, after today, he isn't going to be my boyfriend.

"Kaira?" Mitzi shakes my arm.

I glance down at her hand on me and notice I'm gripping my history book so tight I'm bending the cover.

Something inside me snaps. I stand, knocking over my chair. "I'm not okay. I'm not fucking okay!"

Every head in the class turns in my direction. Guess my internal voice was really my outside voice. The creeping burn of shame torches the lining of my veins as I make my way to the door as fast as possible. I need some air, need to get out of this room.

I need to find Nick and kick his ass.

The door to the classroom doesn't slam behind me when I rush out. "Mitzi, now isn't the time—"

I turn to face her, ready to bitch her out. But the person I fall against is taller, stronger, and far older than my best friend.

"Professor Evans? I-I'm sorry, I—"

"Do you need some help, Ms. Burke?" He gives me a once-over with his astute gaze. For some reason, I don't think it's rude when he cuts me off. It's just him taking control of the situation as if a position of power is something he's used to.

As a professor, I'd say it is.

"No," is the only word I get out before my throat closes up. Hot, fat tears fill my eyes, spill down my cheeks. I bury my face in my hands, too embarrassed to let him see me cry.

With a gentle yet firm grip, Professor Evans pulls my hands from my face. His warm, thick fingertips scratch against my chin when he lifts my gaze to his.

"Are you physically hurt?" he asks. "Did someone touch you?" His voice drops to a dangerous growl and I can't figure out why he'd act so protective.

I shake my head. "He didn't touch me, but I'd like to physically hurt him."

My history teacher tucks a strand of hair behind my ear then drops those same fingers to my neck, his eyes following the movement. His touch—electricity and fire—makes me shiver from tits to toes. I lean into him, wanting more. Needing his comfort.

But needing him, wanting him this way is wrong. Just like Nick cheating. *Wrong.*

Professor Evans must sense my hesitation because he pulls his hand away and squares his shoulders. "Whoever *he* is, he's a fucking idiot."

A giggle breaks through the tears, lightening the moment. "Did you just curse, Professor?"

He crosses his arms, a smirk turning up totally kissable lips. "I may be a professor, but I'm still a man, Ms. Burke."

"I've noticed," I say under my breath. Not under enough, if his full-on grin is any indication.

I wipe my tears then wipe the wet on my jeans before sticking out my hand. "It's Kaira."

He takes mine in his. It's striking how pale my flesh looks against his. I'm not sure I've ever seen anything sexier or more gorgeous.

"John." His thumb rubs my palm. "Nice to officially meet you in a capacity other than your history professor. Though under better circumstances would be my preference."

My mouth opens to tell him it's nice meeting him, too. The door to the classroom bursts open, my best friend tearing through it like a worried hurricane. "I'msosorry-Ishouldn'thavetoldyouhecheated!"

Mitzi speaks so fast that her words jam together, making her almost incoherent. Almost. The word *cheated* came out loud and clear.

The space between John's eyebrows, which a moment ago was smooth, is now furrowed. I swear a flash of anger crosses his handsome face. But it's so quick, I'm not sure it's real. And why would he be mad about my boyfriend cheating? Is he this concerned with all his students?

Jealousy rears its ugly head from somewhere deep inside. I don't want him being this nice and attentive to anyone but me. It's stupid to feel that way, I know. He's probably married.

I risk glancing away from Mitzi to check John's ring finger. It's beautifully barren of gold.

"Did you hear me?" Mitzi grabs my shoulders. I half expect her to shake me.

I step back, out of her grip. "Yeah, I heard you." I know I'm being a dick. Nick cheating is not Mitzi's fault. I just wish she'd told me a different way.

Professor Evans brushes the back of my arm. "I'm going to get back to the classroom. I trust you're in good hands?" He glances at Mitzi.

"The best hands," she answers, and I know that look in her eye. She's trying to figure out what's going on between the two of us.

Nothing, sadly. But maybe it could? Maybe there's something there I never noticed before, my head preoccupied with my cheating boyfriend?

John checks his watch. "I have office hours after class. If you want to stop by, we can continue our discussion, okay?"

A devious and dirty thought enters my mind the moment he offers more time with him. I suddenly know exactly how I'm going to get Nick back for cheating.

"I'd like that. Thank you," I say, making zero attempts to hide the slow smile spreading across my face.

When the door closes behind him, Professor Evans once again inside his classroom, Mitzi drags me down the hall and into the girl's bathroom.

She opens her mouth to speak. I cut her off. "Truth or dare? Isn't that what you were about to ask me?"

Mitzi's eyes bulge and her mouth pops open.

"I pick dare," I forge forward, finally bullying the game to go my way. "After class, you're going to dare me to kiss Professor Evans."

MITZI'S GRIP on my arm is tight, her voice low and hurried. "Are you sure about this?" she asks as her eyes follow Professor Evans out the door. "Maybe we should talk about it first?"

I don't want to talk. I'm sick of talking. That's all we've done in this little game of ours, me too chicken to ever pick dare. No, now it's time for action.

"I'm sure," I say, the statement matching the confidence in my tone. "Dare me."

Mitzi swallows hard, the sound comical and almost lost in the din of students exiting the classroom. "I dare you to kiss Professor Evans."

Pursing my lips, I raise an eyebrow and say, "I accept your challenge."

She turns to leave. Something comes over me, and I grab her arm. "Oh, and tell Nick that I know. Tell him where I am, what you've dared me to do."

I want him to know how it feels when the person you love cheats. I want him to feel what it's like to lose me, and worse, watch me do it with an older, more experienced, far more gorgeous and darker-fleshed man.

Mitzi's face morphs from guilty confusion to righteous indignation. "Yeah, I'll tell him. Hell, I'll walk him there myself."

I give her a quick peck on the cheek and a squeeze. "Thank you. For telling me. For daring me."

Like a spring snapped back into place, Mitzi's entire body relaxes into its more normal state. "We're good?" she asks.

"Better than good."

I head for Professor Evans's office with a devious pep in my step, a juxtaposition to the moping heartbroken way I walked over here after my best friend broke the news before class.

My heart races and blood thunders in my ears as I step up to his door. It's slightly cracked open, but I still raise a shaking hand to knock.

"Come in." Professor Evans—John sounds calm, controlled. How can he be so stoic when I feel like I'm about to catch fire?

The dare was a stupid idea. John offered me a listening ear and his first name. Nothing more. I'm taking advantage of the situation and his kindness. I shouldn't do this. I should go. This is wrong.

"I said, come in, Ms. Burke."

Something about his tone makes me want to comply. I do as I'm told.

Stepping into Professor Evans's office is like stepping into another world. It isn't that the office itself is all that remarkable—bookshelves, messy desk, filing cabinet, two chairs. It's his presence that makes it otherworldly.

He stands, comes around the front of his desk, and stops

inches from me. The spicy scent of his cologne envelops me. For the first time in my life, I feel as if I've bitten off more than I can chew.

I'm not going to get a kiss from this man. I'm not going to get anything from him he doesn't offer. Something instinctual tells me this is how it works with him.

It's the opposite of Nick. He fumbles around my body as if we're still in middle school. And most of the time, I have to beg him for sex. For cuddling. For an ounce of affection.

Why the fuck did I think he was going to marry me? And why the fuck did I think I was going to say yes?

John rolls up the sleeves of his button-down shirt. "Close the door, Ms. Burke."

Again, I do as I'm told.

Using only a hand gesture, he offers me the seat in front of his desk. I take it, but he doesn't take his. Instead, he leans against the desk, his leg against mine. I don't make a move to adjust my position. Neither does he.

After an extended awkward silence, I start to ramble. "Sorry about earlier in class. I'd just found out my boyfriend cheated on me, and I was upset. But you made me feel better. Really good, actually."

I press my palms against my flaming cheeks. They have to be bright red if the temperature is any indication.

"Uh, I don't mean to waste your time. I'm not even sure what I'm doing here."

That's a lie. I'm here on a dare, to get a kiss from my professor. To try out another flavor of life.

John moves closer, something I don't know I want until he does it. He touches my chin as he had in the hallway, bringing my gaze to his. "You know exactly what you're doing here, and you have to know exactly why I asked you to come."

When he says the word *come*, I squeeze my thighs together.

"Why you asked me?" I say, voice tiny and young, just like I am.

He leans in close, so close I can smell the soap he uses. His voice is barely a growl when he says, "Don't you want to get over your soon-to-be ex-boyfriend?"

I do. I do so much.

He chuckles. His breath smells like cinnamon gum.

Wait! Did I say that out loud?

"Stand, Ms. Burke." His command does something to my body. It complies, no longer belonging to me, but longing to be owned by this powerful black stallion. He's the master. I'm a slave.

John switches places with me. Now I'm the one leaning against his desk. When his hands find my hips, he lifts me onto it. My palms find his chest to steady myself. His muscles flex under my touch.

He steps into me. On instinct, I open my legs, let him into my space. With the way he looks at me, touches me, I'm about to get more than a kiss.

"I have a confession," he says, his hands on my bare thighs, exposed because the shorts I'm wearing have ridden up.

I look up at him through thick lashes. "Me, too."

His eyebrow quirks. "You go first."

Excited heat rushes through my bloodstream. I can't believe I'm about to say this. "My best friend dared me to get a kiss from you."

His laugh is sharp and deep. I caught him by surprise. Before I can say anything else or die of embarrassment, he grabs the back of my neck and brings my face to his. "I think I can help you with that."

Everything about this man overpowers me when his lips

move over mine. His tongue darts out to play, and I answer in kind.

The kiss is everything I imagined, and so much more than I knew a kiss could be. It's as if the act of making love, or fucking, starts with the penetration of the mouth.

Breathless, I pull back, my vision a bit blurred. "Wh-what's your confession?"

With his dark brown eyes locked on mine, he says, "I've wanted to fuck you from the moment you walked into my classroom. Teach you a lesson that has nothing to do with history."

I draw in a sharp breath, my mouth popping open, my eyes bulging wide. "Y-You've wanted *me*?" I don't understand it, but I'm sure in fuck not going to question it. In truth, I've wanted him, too. I've been too stuck on Nick, too wrapped up in myself to pursue it.

"I want to make something clear before we start." He runs his lips up the side of my neck to my ear. "This has nothing to do with your grade, and we can stop at any time."

I nod to let him know I understand. "I don't want to stop," I admit.

Now it's his turn to nod. His fingers unbutton my shorts, slide down the zipper. "Lift your ass." When I do, he glides my shorts off, lets them fall to the floor.

His hand cups my shaved mound. The feral noise he makes soaks me. "You aren't wearing panties, you naughty little white-trash slut."

A jolt of lust rushes through me at the term. The politically correct feminist in me wants to be offended. But the way he uses it is so *hot*. I *want* to be his white-trash slut.

"I am naughty," I say, my voice taking on an innocent tone. "Maybe you want to punish me?"

I have no idea where this dirty talk is coming from, but I like it.

He pulls his hand from my cunt and sniffs it. "Don't worry, Kaira. I'm going to punish this little pink pussy soon enough. First, I'm going to taste you, see if the reality lives up to my fantasy."

His fantasy? So he's been thinking about me, too?

The door to the office bursts open. A red-faced Nick rushes in, panting as if he ran from the dorms over here. Maybe he did.

"Kaira, I'm sorry. I—"

It takes Nick a moment to realize what he's seeing. When he does, his fists clench at his side, and I swear his face grows redder. That can't be good for his blood pressure.

I expect Professor Evans to push away from me, deny whatever this looks like. Try to play it off. That doesn't happen.

"Close the door," John says to Nick, his voice smooth like silk and strong like steel.

To my surprise, Nick does what he's told. He doesn't shout obscenities. Doesn't demand to know what's happening. Doesn't storm out and threaten to go to the school officials. Like a whipped puppy, he complies. It's almost as if seeing me like this turns him on in a way I've never seen before. The bulge in his pants is a dead giveaway.

"Take a seat." John kicks the chair I was sitting in toward Nick. It stops just far enough away to give us space while still giving Nick prime viewing.

"Yeah," Nick says. "O-Okay. I can sit."

"I was just about to eat your girlfriend's pussy," he says to Nick.

"Ex-girlfriend," I correct.

Nick acts like he's going to stand. "Wait, Kaira. I don't want that. I can explain. It was a stupid mistake."

"I said *sit*." There's zero room in John's tone for interpretation. He's the one in charge here.

Nick settles into the chair, folds his hands on his lap, across his hard dick. He isn't hiding anything. Not that there's much there to hide.

John glances at me, a devious grin on his gorgeous face. "Since this is what I do best," he says to Nick, "I'm going to teach you how to properly eat a juicy peach. You good with that, *son?*"

Nick's knuckles are white as he grips the chair. "Yeah."

John shoots him a glare. Nick hastily corrects, "Yes, sir."

John turns his back on Nick until he's facing me. "This okay with you?" he mouths so Nick won't hear.

Okay? *Okay?* This is way fucking better than okay. Nick's about to watch me get eaten and fucked by an intelligent, experienced, older man. Not just any man. A black man. If Nick has any qualms about that, he knows better than to show it.

I nod in answer to John's question.

Using my hips for leverage, John pushes me further back onto his desk. "Lean back," he instructs. Like a good student, I obey.

I prop myself up on my elbows. I want to watch, just like Nick's watching.

Taking his time, refusing to rush, Professor Evans explores every line and crease. His rough hot tongue laps at my clit then pushes into my folds until it finds my center. My ass lifts off the desk, and he grabs it to hold me there.

Everything about what he's doing feels amazing. Faster than I've ever been able to before, I feel the tidal shift of an impending orgasm. Where Nick is sloppy and lazy, John is practiced and precise. Every flick, every ounce of pressure is measured. Purposeful.

"Oh, God," I say through panting breaths. I'm close. So fucking close.

John must sense the shift. He isn't willing to let me get off yet. He pulls back so abruptly that I fall onto the desk with a thud. I'm about to whine my displeasure when he does something else that surprises me. He slaps my cunt. Hard.

"Ouch!" I react. It fucking hurts, but it also feels good. More blood rushes south, further swelling my plump lips.

"You see that?" John says to Nick.

Wide-eyed, Nick nods.

"You see how she's breathing? How swollen her pink pussy is?"

"Y-yes, sir."

John stands, walks over to Nick, and drags him out of the chair by his shirt. John moves with the grace of a predator. Nick stumbles over his own feet.

"No, I don't think you can see," John says, shoving Nick's face in my crotch. "Look at your woman. Look at how she opens for me."

On cue, I spread my legs wider.

"Look at how her flower blossoms under the right kind of care. Take time to smell the roses, *son*." John takes a deep breath of my sweet cunt. Nick follows suit.

Pressing his dark thumb against my pink clit, John says to Nick, "And don't forget to water the plants."

Without warning, John's massive fingers plunge inside me. He's two wide, which might as well be four wide. But the instant he hits the nub deep inside me, I wouldn't care if he shoved his entire fist in there. All I can feel is pleasure.

My orgasm takes me by surprise, pop-quiz style. It shoots out of me, a warm wet mess that soaks John's chin, his shirt, and the floor.

"Mmm, that's it," John encourages between slurps as he drinks me in. "Squirt for me, baby girl. Squirt hard."

Like I've done from the moment I walked in his office, I do what he says. My vision blackens around the edges, my throat hurts from screaming, and my muscles can no longer hold me up, but I don't care. I don't care about anything. I'm in heaven, and nothing will bring me crashing back to earth.

Not a cheating boyfriend or the fact I know this kind of pleasure can't last.

"Oh my God." Nick sounds shocked. He also sounds like a complete wimp. "I've never seen her do that before."

"That's because you don't know what you're doing," I manage to say. "Haven't bothered learning."

John claps Nick on the shoulder, wipes some of my pussy juice off on him in the process. "That's why I'm here, to teach you how to get it done. That is if she'll take you back after you've cheated."

John helps me sit up. I lean against his chest but stare at Nick.

"I want to learn," Nick says. The look on his face tells me he means it. "I want you back, and I'm willing to do anything to prove it."

Nick's eyes flick from me to Professor Evans and back.

Is Nick saying what I think he's saying?

"Go on, then." John faces his hips toward Nick and points to his zipper. "Prove it."

With shaking hands, Nick unzips the professor's pants.

"Pull it out," John says.

I watch, fascinated, as my maybe ex-boyfriend pulls out my new lover's cock. Anaconda is more like it. Nick's face must match mine. I had no idea a cock could be that huge. Apparently, neither had Nick.

"Now suck it." John's command is sobering. Nick had no idea what he was walking into when he burst through the door. Neither had I.

The thought of watching my cheating boyfriend suck a huge black cock makes something inside me sing with delight. I want him to feel humiliated. Like he's less of a man, because he is.

"And do a good job, babe," I tease as I stroke the thick hard length of my professor. "You want to win me back, don't you?"

Nick falls to his knees, wraps both of his hands around the base of the huge, dark member spearing toward his face. Tentatively, he sticks his tongue out, tastes the precum beaded on the head.

Impatient, I grab a fistful of Nick's dirty blond hair and shove his face onto John's cock. Nick gags, his body bucking for air. I hold him in place. John grins his approval.

Finally, I let go, let Nick find his own pace. I climb off the desk, get eye-level with all the action, and let myself really get into it.

"You look so good with a big black dick in your mouth, babe." I kiss Nick's cheek, stroke his hair. "You're doing such a good job proving to me that you want me back."

Spit slides down Nick's chin, drips onto the jeans covering his thighs. He chokes, acts like he's going to pull off. "Nuh, uh." I push his head back down. When I do, John's eyes roll back, his head facing the ceiling.

"What do you think, Professor?" I ask as I stand, wrap my arms around John's shoulders, and bring my lips to his.

"He isn't bad, for an inexperienced white boy." He kisses me, and I yield to him. "But I don't want his mouth to finish me. I want your creamy-white cunt."

I tap Nick on the head to let him know to stop. He pulls off with a popping sound that makes my pussy clench.

"Stay there," John instructs Nick as he turns me so my ass is facing him. He pushes me over his desk, exposing my holes. "Watch and learn."

From over my shoulder, I watch as John rubs his slick head against my opening. When he finds it, he pauses at the entrance, lets me get used to his girth.

Grabbing Nick by the back of the head, John brings him

in close, until Nick's nose touches my ass. "I want to make sure you can see me fuck your girl. Stretch her tight walls until she's so loose she won't even feel you inside her. She'll have to come back to me for another taste of real pleasure."

The thought of doing this again, with them both, sets me on fire. "I want to come," I beg. "And I want to come back for more."

John pushes further inside, only an inch. Might as well be a mile. Fuck, that hurts. My whimpers tell him so.

"Let's get through the first time, baby girl," he says before grabbing two handfuls of my milky-white ass in his dark mahogany hands. The contrast is so beautiful, I could look at him against me all day.

He lifts and pulls my ass apart, causing everything to stretch with the strain. I gasp and grab onto the other side of the desk as he slides in further.

"Remember to breathe and relax," he coaches me. His thumb strokes my puckered asshole. I'm not sure if it's meant as a distraction or a promise of something yet to come. Next time.

"Oh, hell." It's Nick that says the same words stuck in my throat.

"Looks good, doesn't it?" John asks.

Nick's eyes lock with mine. "Babe, you should see how stretched you are. How swollen. I've never seen anything so fucking divine."

"Taste it," John prompts before shoving Nick's face against my stretched pussy with John's dick still inside.

I can barely feel the heat from Nick's tongue mixed in with the heat of everything else. This is easily the hottest thing I've ever done, and I want more.

"How's that taste?" John demands.

"Good, sir," Nick answers.

"Now watch, *son*, and learn as I fuck this pussy the way a real man should."

John does just that. His hard, thick, black length pounds into my tight white pussy. I hold onto the desk and scream as I release, over and over and over again.

"That's it, baby girl." John smacks my ass, watches it jiggle, his thumb still planted firmly against my asshole. "That's it. Come all over my dick. Squeeze me nice and tight so I can fill you up."

"Please fill me," I beg. "Don't you want him to fill me?" I say to Nick.

He nods and licks his lips. "Y-Yeah, I do. Please, sir. Please fill my girlfriend's cunt with your come."

"This is the only way, baby," I say to Nick. "The only way you get me back."

"I'm ready," John says to both of us. "You ready for me to fill this pussy?"

"Yes," Nick and I both say at the same time.

John picks up the pace and I feel like I might split apart. "Yeah, that's it. So tight. So fucking tight."

Wet slapping noises fill the room along with the scent of our sex.

"Such a good slut," John encourages. "Such a tight slut."

"I'm your slut," I say.

"Your slut," Nick pants in agreement. He sounds as excited as I am, sounds like he's about to come, and no one's even touching his little dick.

"Here it comes," John announces. "Here. It. *Comes*."

The explosion of hot seed from the professor's cock is violent. His molten cream fills me, seeps out the sides, runs down my legs.

John pumps a few more times then holds himself deep inside. We're both breathing hard. It takes a minute to regulate.

Slowly, agonizingly, the professor pulls his spent dick from my sore and abused cunt.

"Get over here," I hear John say to Nick. The next thing I feel is Nick's mouth on my pussy, on my asshole. "Clean it up. All of it."

Nick makes slurping noises. He's never eaten me this enthusiastically. Maybe what he needed all along was another man to show him how. To take control. To give him a job to do.

John strokes my back as Nick cleans my cunt of every last drop of come. I squirm under sensation overload, moan when Nick hums against my sore flesh.

"That was perfect," John whispers as he kisses up my neck and over my shoulders.

"Mmm, yeah. Perfect," I purr.

"She's clean," Nick says to John from his position on his knees, beneath us both. Where he belongs.

John checks his watch. "Office hours are over. You should get dressed," he says to me. "Pick up her shorts," he says to Nick.

Nick does what he's told. From now on, that's how it'll always be.

I use his head to steady myself as I step one foot then the other into my shorts. When he glides them up my legs, he grins, his lips still wet and sticky from my pussy juice mixed with come.

"Okay, fine." I roll my eyes, throw my blonde hair over my shoulder. "I won't dump you. But only if we come back and do this again."

I glance at the professor, eyes hopeful. I'd flat out beg if he made me.

John chuckles. "I have office hours every Tuesday and Thursday."

"It's settled then." I saunter over to John, throw my arms

around him, and kiss the sweet mouth that gave me so much pleasure. "See you next week, Professor."

"Next week it is," he replies, a smirk tilting up luscious lips. "I dare you to miss our appointment."

THE END
Get Access to over 20 more FREE Erotica Downloads at Shameless Book Deals

Shameless Book Deals is a website that shamelessly brings you the very best erotica at the best prices from the best authors to your inbox every day. Sign up to our newsletter to get access to the daily deals and the Shameless Free Story Archive!

SHAMELESS BOOK DEALS

The best place to get erotica recommendations tailored to you! Sign up for the newsletter below and find out why it's so good to be shameless! Free stories for subscribers.

Newsletter Sign Up

∾

Pseudo-Incest

Satisfy the Man of the House (Ten Brats who Give him Anything he Wants): These brats can pout all they want, they are going to satisfy the man of the house, even if what he demands is to take them hard and most certainly without using protection or pulling out. These stories are totally taboo and will leave you panting!

∾

Gangbang/Menage

Taken 54 Times (54 Men. 10 Women. You Do The Math): How many could you handle? Two? Three? A dozen muscular athletes? How about trying all fifty-four? The women in these ten stories are taken hard every which way and just when they think it's over, there's another man who is just beginning. They are left messy, panting and oh so satisfied!

∾

Pseudo-Incest

Owned by the Man of the House (Ten Brats who Learn how to Please Him): The man of the house lays claim to everything *in* his house, and that includes these precious little brats who think that they can get away with flaunting their perfect fertile bodies in front of him. When he decides to take what is his, he's going to take his pleasure **hard, unprotected and all night long**. They'll find how difficult it is to maintain a princess-pout when they're screaming his name.

～

Light BDSM

Shameless Submission (Ten Perfect Princesses Bend to his Will): True Masters come from all walks of life, some of them are the very pillars of our society, some of them are in our own homes. What they all have in common is that when they choose you as their submissive, you're left writhing in ecstasy, bent to their will, and life will never be the same again.

～

Pseudo-Incest

Ravished by the Man of the House (Ten Brats who Learn How to Please Him): Those perfect pouts have been getting these little princesses everything they wanted for years. Now, for the first time, all they're getting is into the best kind of trouble with the Man of the House. They are going to be left a sweaty mess, legs quivering too hard to stand, and full of his special gift.

～

E-Rom

Just Because You Love Me (Ten Bite-Size Spicy Love Stories): These stories go to show that just because you're in love doesn't mean you can't get it **hard**, it simply means you also get to cuddle afterwards. The women in this set are left with quivering legs, but whether that's because of the magic words or because of more... physical means is hard to decide!

～

Pseudo-Incest

<u>Pounded by the Man of the House (Ten Untouched
Princesses Who Learn How To Please Him)</u>: These beautiful
brats may have fantasies of their virginity being taken by
gentle lovemaking on their wedding night... but those are all
pounded away as the men of their houses teach them how to
really please a man.

~

Dubious Consent

*T*aking Advantage (Ten Perfect Princesses
Overwhelmed by Him): Their beauty has allowed
them to take so much from this world. Doors are opened for
them, favors are granted, gifts are given. Now it's time for
these princesses to be overwhelmed, taken advantage of and
have their legs opened for a very insistent gift that won't take
no for an answer...

~

Pseudo-Incest

LUSTING for the Man of the House (Ten Untouched Princess
Who Get What He Wants): These sexy brats have an itch that
only the man of the house can scratch. They can't hold themselves back any longer, they *need* to give everything to the
one man who makes them so wet they can't think straight.

***

Anal

The Tradesman's Entrance (Ten New Housewives who let

Him in the Back Door): These sexy young housewives thought being a kept woman would be a dream come true, but while their husbands are away, they still have... needs. When the tradesmen come knocking these housewives fall under the spell of those rippling muscles. When rough hands bend them over, they only fight back a little, they need to give him what he wants... something nobody has ever taken from them before...

≈

Dubious Consent

TAKING Advantage 2 (Ten Perfect Princesses Overwhelmed by Him): Ten more untouchable princesses learn who is in charge. Taken, used, utterly betrayed by their own bodies they are victims of their own lust no matter how much they deny it.

≈

Pseudo-Incest

BROKEN in by the Man of the House (Ten Untouched Princess Who Get What He Wants): The man of the house is laying claim to all the fertile brats in his house. Even though it's SO WRONG, these untouched princesses are going to take what he gives them and love every dirty second of it.

≈

Lactation

SHAMELESS LACTATION (Ten Fertile Beauties Overflowing

with Creamy Goodness): The women in this bundle are so full of creamy goodness they're almost bursting with the need for release. Lucky for them there's no shortage of eager men eager to latch on and drink their sweet nectar.

~

Pseudo-Incest

USED by the Man of the House (Ten Bratty Princesses get that Pout Wiped off Their Faces by Him): The bratty princesses in this bundle are so incredibly innocent, they don't realize how their tight fertile bodies drive the men of their houses wild with lust. It's only so long before he has to take what is his, hard and unprotected.

~

Interracial/Cuckold

TAKEN in Front of Him (Ten Tight Princesses Stretched by the Black Bull): Each of these tight white princesses can't help but wonder what it would be like to get stretched out by that big black bull. They can't resist, their men are going to have to watch every long thrust, hear every shrieking climax, learn what how much they love being ridden hard by a *real* man.